Dear Reader:

In response to your enthusiasm for Candlelight Ecstasy Romances, we are now increasing the number of titles per month from two to three.

We are pleased to offer you sensuous novels set in America depicting modern American women and men as they confront the provocative problems of a modern relationship.

Throughout the history of the Candlelight line, Dell has tried to maintain a high standard of excellence, to give you the finest in reading pleasure. It is now and will remain our most ardent ambition.

Vivian Stephens
Editor
Candlelight Romances

THE MARRIAGE SEASON

Sally Dubois

A CANDLELIGHT ECSTASY ROMANCE

Published by
Dell Publishing Co., Inc.
1 Dag Hammarskjold Plaza
New York, New York 10017

Dell ® TM 681510, Dell Publishing Co., Inc.

ISBN: 0-440-16058-8

Printed in the United States of America

First printing—June 1981

ONE

Julia doubted that anyone, even Dr. Arokiaswamy's son, could be as wonderful as Leela claimed.

"He was so very lively and affectionate when he was small." Leela spoke softly in her Tamil accent with rolled r's and curled l's, overlaid with a British staccato. "Joseph is a good boy; it is to say he is a good man."

Julia's smile brought dimples to her cheeks—peaches and cream cheeks Aunt Frances called them. And with her sable hair pulled back in a braided bun, she looked like a ballerina slightly flushed from dancing. "He sounds like a very fine person." She pictured a skinny Indian man with microscope glasses reading the fine print of a medical book—yes, a goody-goody.

"You will see when he returns from America," said Leela in a decisive voice which matched her matronly figure and hair streaked with steel gray.

Julia turned her head to look out the window as the train moved slowly into the Madras station. Raman, Leela's husband, was busy taking down the luggage from the rack above their heads. Outside, the chorus of vendors could be heard over the train's roar—a ragamuffin girl with a tray of bright flowers at her hip, calling out her wares, *"pu pu pu pu pu"*; a tenor with a tray of coffee, *"kapi . . . kapi";* and an old, bare-chested man with tea, calling in his toadlike voice, *"te te te te."*

Julia kept her gaze away from Leela. "Well, I probably won't be here to see him anyway," she said with a sigh.

"Do not worry," soothed Leela. "We will try. Some way you will be able to stay at the clinic. And certainly you must meet Joseph."

Julia couldn't care less if she met Joseph, but she didn't want to offend Leela by expressing that sentiment openly. She turned to Leela with a renewed smile. "Well, at least I did accomplish something. I learned quite a lot about India and I did find my mother's orphanage. That's what I always wanted to do. I sure was lucky the Peace Corps assigned me to Tamil Nadu, as I requested, instead of some other state in India, or some other country for that matter."

"It is too bad they did not remember much your mother at the convent."

"Isn't it funny they remembered my grandparents so well when they came to adopt her, but they couldn't remember my mother."

"It is understandable that rich Americans would stand out clearly, and there would have been so many little girls."

"My grandparents were hardly rich—they were farmers taking the one big trip of their lives, but then they must have impressed the nuns as being quite worldly." With a wistful smile she pictured the scene vividly, as if she had been there—her grandmother, middle-aged, dressed in her Sunday best with hat and gloves, hugging a little Tamil girl in an oversized, hand-me-down dress, while the nuns watched with clasped hands and satisfied smiles.

"You were hoping to find relatives here in India, is it not?" asked Leela.

"Not really. Of course it would've been nice if the nuns had known something. It would've given me some real connection to India. Even when my parents were alive I didn't really think of my mother as Indian. My father used to call her his Spanish beauty." Julia's brown eyes sparkled at the memory. "So I guess if I'd found relatives here it would've made me feel more like I belong."

"But I feel you are related to me. You are like a daughter. I so wanted a girl."

"I thought you always wanted a son, the way you speak of Joseph so often." Julia felt a small twitch of jealousy as she spoke his name.

"A son is a necessity, but I very much wished for a daughter."

The train lurched to a halt.

"We shall have to find some decent hotel before we go for medical supplies," said Raman. Though he had the wrinkles and grayness of a man in his late fifties, and was well-respected as the clinic's accountant, his voice lacked the strength to command others. "Will you take this one?" he asked Julia softly, indicating the small suitcase.

"Yes, of course." She stood up and pulled at the loose end of her peacock blue sari to make sure it was draped properly over her shoulder, then picked up the suitcase.

"We must go to the Lakshmi Hotel," said Leela. "Julia is to meet friends there."

"Yes, Peace Corps friends," explained Julia, "but it isn't that important."

"No, no, the Lakshmi is a good hotel," insisted Raman. "We shall go there."

As soon as they stepped down from the train, a porter grabbed their luggage—with hardly a word from Raman —and placed one suitcase on his head and held the other in his hand. They followed him, almost obediently, as he wove a way through the crowd. When they emerged from the darkness of the station into the sunlight outside, Julia marveled at the kaleidoscope confronting them: Bright saris in every festival color; matrons laden with gold jewelry; and among the cars and buses, white bullocks with magnificently curved horns swaying their heads gently in figure eights as they pulled wooden, two-wheeled carts. City life—it always seemed exciting to those fresh from the countryside. And Madras, thought Julia, appeared as a multifaceted jewel of a city.

Raman hailed a taxi and within minutes they were in the courtyard of the Lakshmi Hotel. Raman went to inquire about rooms and Leela opened the door on her side of the taxi to let the breeze trickle through and allay the stifling heat.

After the driver got out to wait in the shade of a neem tree, Leela turned to Julia. "When Joseph comes, he will be able to help at the clinic. That will give relief to Dr. Arokiaswamy, and to us nurses as well. Then after the doctor retires this year, Joseph could take over his practice."

"Is he really coming?" asked Julia, trying to conceal her lack of interest. "Did Dr. Arokiaswamy say so? I haven't heard one word about it except from you, and then Nirmala keeps hoping." She thought of Dr. Arokiaswamy's daughter, Nirmala, who talked about her brother in a half-bragging, half-affectionate tone.

"The doctor is not sure of his son. He said nothing, it is true, but I know he will come. I know him. He will at least come for Nirmala's wedding."

"So that's why you're talking about him so much these days. Well, if he does come for the wedding, I guess I'll meet him after all."

A hotel servant in a khaki uniform mysteriously ap-

10

peared with coffee. He handed out stainless steel tumblers and left. Leela continued. "You will like him. It is good that you both should meet."

Julia laughed. "Trying to fix me up?" She had become accustomed to Leela's proddings about marriage.

"He would be a very suitable husband," offered Leela.

Julia, her hand wrapped around the warm tumbler, sipped the sweet, milky coffee with satisfaction. "I'm sure he would. And I'm sure Dr. and Mrs. Arokiaswamy will be making arrangements for him to marry some woman in their caste." Then she added with a slightly theatrical voice, "And as for my part, I would never consider marrying anyone unless I knew him . . . and loved him." She stopped herself from further adding that she was quite certain she wouldn't even like Joseph.

"You young people do not know what is love," Leela replied in friendly criticism. "My husband and I met only once before marriage, when his family and relatives came to see me. Now we have been married thirty-one years, a happy marriage. And if you were to marry a man like Joseph, then you could stay at the clinic."

Julia's lighthearted tone took on a more serious note. "I only want to stay on as a nurse, not get married. And even if I did want to get married—which I don't—I wouldn't marry for such motives. There'd have to be love."

"Of course. There should be affection. That will develop over time. But do not shut off your mind to marriage."

Leela didn't understand, thought Julia finishing the coffee. Her marriage had been arranged and it had worked out well. Leela would have no idea what Julia had gone through with men—from Hank smashing her sand castle in the sixth grade, to Roy virtually attacking her after the senior prom, to Stephen jilting her for a highly paid fashion model, while she struggled with first-year nursing

11

courses. Certainly decent, sensitive men did exist, but Julia had yet to meet one who had those qualities and at the same time could rouse her romantic instincts.

"I'm just not very interested in marriage at this point," said Julia. "I have my career as a nurse, and besides, men are nothing but trouble."

"Not all men. Some are good," replied Leela. "That is why it is necessary for older people to find the right match for younger people. They know who will be proper."

"And you think Joseph's proper?" Julia's tone held amusement. She thought this Joseph must be an absolute bore to be such a wonderful fellow in Leela's judgment. And besides, he must be a spoiled brat, having not only loving parents, but Leela doting over him as well.

"Definitely he is proper. The girl he marries will be a very fortunate girl."

The servant reappeared to collect the empty tumblers, and as he left, Raman joined them. In a quiet voice he said, "There are no rooms available. We did not remember it is the marriage season. They thought it would be very difficult to find any vacancies in Madras, especially this late in the afternoon. I telephoned some other places."

"At least the Queen's Palace Hotel should have rooms," said Leela.

The Queen's Palace registered on Julia's mind from past experiences—old, run down, overpriced.

"I thought that also," said Raman. "I telephoned and it seems we might have luck over there."

They drove two blocks and pulled through a high archway into another courtyard, one full of tropical plants and trees. Raman went into the hotel office and Leela went to buy flowers. She returned in a few minutes with a plantain leaf packet tied with pink string. Then Raman returned; this time his face looked worried.

12

"They do have rooms, but we must wait here one hour before they are to be ready."

"But the store will close in an hour and tomorrow is Saturday." It was unnecessary for Julia to say it; they all knew the problem. The clinic needed more medical supplies by Monday. It couldn't wait for the regular shipment in two weeks. Normally they would have ordered them by mail, but coming to Madras gave them a chance to do some shopping and enjoy the big city. The idea that they wouldn't reach the store in time hadn't occurred to them.

Julia offered what she thought was the only logical solution. "Maybe I should wait here with the luggage while you and Leela pick up the supplies."

"That will not be wise to leave you here alone," replied Raman.

Leela added, "It is not proper, a young girl alone in a hotel."

Julia felt mildly irritated by their overprotectiveness, especially now when it got in the way of important work. And, after all, she was twenty-three, hardly a baby. "I can assure you that I'll be perfectly all right. I insist."

Julia's firm tone settled the matter. They unloaded the dicky, the car's trunk, and took the luggage into the hotel lobby. Julia sat down in a teak armchair with a caned seat and back, and Raman arranged the luggage near her feet. Then he switched on the ceiling fan which did little more than stir up the heat.

"Are you certain you will be all right sitting here alone?" asked Leela while Raman surveyed the lobby with a fatherly and suspicious eye.

"Of course. I feel quite comfortable." She smiled at all their worry, even though the cameo-shaped gaps on the walls where the dark green paint had peeled off did give the room a slightly eerie touch.

13

"We will return shortly," said Leela. She handed Julia the plantain leaf packet and they left.

Alone and enjoying the bright patch of sunlight in front of her created by the small ceiling window, Julia untied the packet. From it she pulled out a long chain of jasmine blossoms, which looked like a string of snowy white popcorn. The exotic perfume, heavy and rich, and not at all subtle, delighted Julia. It had become a familiar and welcome fragrance.

Doubling the chain, she fastened it in a semi-circle around the right side of her dark brown bun. If she had known someone had emerged from a hotel room off the lobby and was watching her from the nearby shadows, she wouldn't have reveled in this small pleasure. But she didn't see the stranger.

What she did see as she turned her head to fasten the flowers was a statue of the Virgin Mary on a shelf above the door. She knew it meant that Christians owned the hotel, just as a Hindu goddess would have indicated that Hindus owned it. She gazed at the statue for some time before her eyes quite suddenly dropped to the darkness of the doorway below, as if pulled by some magnet.

Leaning against the frame with folded bronze arms was a tall, broad-shouldered man in a black knit shirt and off-white pants. His hair falling across his forehead seemed blacker than that of most Indians, blacker than midnight, thought Julia with a catch in her throat.

He could have been a Greek sailor with his Mediterranean complexion, except that his eyes, which magnetically pulled her gaze back to them, had a leaf shape, not quite Oriental and not quite Western. She imagined Genghis Khan would have had such eyes, with their commanding stare.

Despite herself, Julia's initial response was interest, but

almost immediately—as soon as she could regain her wits—she tensed. How long had he been staring at her? This was a land of such multilayered reality and imagery. She should have had keener vision. He seemed to envelop and claim her with his eyes. She detested it and wished she hadn't been so hasty in sending Raman and Leela away. Why had she scoffed at what she had thought was only a formality of concern? They were absolutely right. A young, and she might add, foolish girl should not sit alone in a hotel, at least not an Indian hotel. Of course there was no real danger, but the situation did create a discomforting tension.

Now, as a result of her stubbornness, Julia was helplessly trapped, having to guard the luggage. To make matters worse, she was sitting so close to the sunlight—it touched the bottom edge of her sari—that her face and arms seemed to glow. She could be seen clearly in that spotlight, while he stood almost hidden by the darkness.

Two years ago, during her nurses' training in Milwaukee, she hadn't thought much of it when male patients had given her the eye or had been a little too suggestive in their banter. She would sweetly but firmly handle them, and shrug it off as an occupational hazard. But she had become very sensitive since coming to India, where any type of male attention was considered insulting.

Julia felt the man's stare burning her skin, though she had turned her gaze away from him almost immediately. She blushed at the thought that before becoming aware of his presence she had been looking in his direction at the statue above his head. *Damn it,* she cursed silently, biting her lip, *he probably thinks I was staring at him.* And she hated it when she blushed. Her already peach cheeks bloomed like brilliant roses.

Each minute of this humiliation seemed to drag very

15

slowly, until she noticed a fellow Peace Corps worker amble up to the hotel desk. After a few words with the clerk, he spotted Julia and walked over. His sunburn was redder than his strawberry blond hair.

"Hey, Julia," he said in his offhanded drawl.

"Hi, Harry. Did Rick and Jean come? Did you get rooms at the Lakshmi?"

"Yeah, we all came this morning and I think we got the last rooms at the Lakshmi. When you didn't show, we figured you might be at the Queen's Palace. I tell you, with the marriage season in full swing and tourists arriving in hordes, it's really tough to get a room in town."

"Yes. We tried the Lakshmi and now we're even having trouble getting rooms here." Julia was still nervously aware of the man in the doorway. "So, any plans for today?" she asked, trying to ease the tightness in her throat.

"Would ya believe they're having a band here tonight—trying to attract the tourists, I guess. I came over to check up on it."

"That sounds nice." Her voice lacked enthusiasm. She didn't really care to dance with Harry, even though she had made it clear from the beginning that any advances on his part would be totally wasted. She would much rather go to the movies than be held in Harry's arms. For now, however, she had a more immediate problem, which made her want to involve him in conversation and detain him as long as possible. "So . . . how's life in your village?"

"Oh, that same old woman is blaming the drought on me. 'Ever since you came this happened or that happened,' she says. Sometimes I think the whole Peace Corps idea is a waste, trying to put new ideas on people who don't really want them—except in your case, I suppose."

The man staring at Julia began to fade into the background of her mind. She made the mental and emotional transition from the Indian world to the American world. "I don't know if I'm that much help," she said, trying to be polite. In truth she had been of more help than she had anticipated. The clinic always needed extra nurses, but apart from helping out at the clinic, she had started a nurses' training program, had conducted health education workshops for the villagers, and had often helped Leela and the other nurses with simple doctoring when Dr. Arokiaswamy was away. And still Julia felt there would be no end to the work she could do at the Tamaraiyur clinic.

"I guess it'll all be over in a month," said Harry. "The first thing I'm going to do when I get back is order a big, juicy steak in an air-conditioned restaurant. Say, how's it coming with you? You were trying to work out something so you could stay."

"It looks fairly hopeless at this point," sighed Julia. "They do need me, but it doesn't look like the government will give the clinic another nurse's position, especially since they're giving it another doctor's position. I'll really hate to leave."

"What about your parents?" he asked. "Won't you be glad to see them?"

Julia looked at him with a quizzical frown. "They died in an auto accident when I was eleven."

"Oh, yeah, you told me. Then what about your aunt and uncle?"

"We were never very close." Such a difference, thought Julia, between her aunt and uncle and Leela and Raman. Aunt Frances was a career woman, a buyer for a chain of department stores. They had never wanted children, and had taken Julia in as an undesired duty. Leela and Raman, by contrast, had always wanted children, but couldn't have them. To compensate, they showered their love on other people's children, and had practically adopted Julia, in heart and spirit, if not legally.

"I don't know," drawled Harry. "It seems like it'd be awfully difficult, this staying on in India. I don't know . . ."

"Yes, I'd miss my friends and a lot of things, and there *are* difficulties." Julia's awareness of the man in the doorway heightened. She shot a quick glance in his direction. He still stood there. "But I feel there's so much to be done here. I guess I feel useful and wanted." She didn't mention how enthralled she was by India.

Harry started to leave abruptly, not in the Indian way to which she had grown accustomed—lingering conversation, delays, staving off the inevitable separation. "Well, see ya later," he said brusquely.

"Wait!" said Julia with a sudden shudder. "Why don't you stay awhile and have some Limca with me?"

"Got to go. Said I'd meet Jean and Rick at Moor Market and I'm running late now." Harry walked out of the hotel lobby with his usual stride.

Julia was now alone with *him,* thrust suddenly back into the Indian world. That Harry, she scolded silently, always in a hurry. Why hadn't she told him about the situation? Because he wouldn't have felt it was a situation. He probably would have scoffed at the idea. And when she thought about it from an American perspective, she couldn't understand why she thought of it as a situation either. She only knew that she felt disconcerted, more than she ever had when other ruffians had stared at her.

Slowly she glanced around at the doorway. He had gone. She sighed with relief, then started when from her other side came a soft, deep voice with only a slight Tamil accent.

18

"What a lovely apparition."

She knew who it was without looking. Her whole body tensed. And yet his remark had been so uncharacteristic. It rang sweetly in her ears.

"Pardon me," he said gently, "I just returned from America today and was sleeping. I couldn't remember where I was, or whether I was just dreaming when I saw you."

Although she knew that by speaking to her he was treating her as an American—he would never speak that way to an Indian woman he didn't know—she decided to respond in the Indian way with stone silence. Hopefully that would discourage him.

Almost in response to her thoughts he said, "I heard you speaking to the American man, and then I realized you were also American. You wear the sari so perfectly, and the jasmine flowers. The way you put them in your hair . . ."

Julia pressed her lips firmly together. He was becoming a little too familiar, at least by Indian standards, and she felt determined to maintain those standards with this disturbing man. She wasn't about to explain that she actually was half Indian and trap herself in a conversation with him.

He continued with a hint of sorrow in his voice. "It reminded me of my mother and sister. I haven't seen them for six years."

Julia sighed and relaxed her shoulders a little. She looked up at him. The angular lines and roughness of his unshaven face—a ruthlessly handsome face—contrasted with the trace of pain in his dark eyes, the sensitive eyes of a Mughal conqueror. Julia's breath caught at her poetic contrast. Up close he didn't seem the shallow rogue. Instead he was a vital man who perhaps had suffered, who

19

perhaps could feel. She relented in her judgment. Maybe he hadn't been staring at her in that wrong way.

"Is it not strange," he said, continuing the one-sided conversation, "the first woman I see when I return from America is an American. May I ask your name?" He smiled, and Julia detected a natural confidence in his voice.

"I don't see that it's any of your business," she replied curtly.

A flash of surprise grazed his face and he arched his brows. She suddenly regretted her words. His tone of voice, his apparent intentions, all seemed quite sincere, not in the least mocking or lewd. And it wasn't like her to be harsh, even in America, but certainly not here in India, where people were so very sensitive.

She hoped her American flippancy hadn't hurt him, but before she could make amends, he smiled, flashing his strong white teeth, and said, "Hmm, quite a long name." A smile tugged at the corners of Julia's mouth, but she controlled it. "I am Selvam, and your name must be Mary?" He paused and when there was no response, asked, "Linda? No? Perhaps Suzanne?"

She imagined he was throwing out the names of past girl friends, those he had conquered. It wasn't difficult to imagine that many girls would have been captivated by his strong magnetism, which despite Julia's effort to resist also affected her. Afraid he would continue on and on down the list, and hoping to get rid of him, she said, "Julia."

"Of course," he said with deliberation. "I should have guessed. . . ." His voice trailed off into some deep thought. Then he spoke with force. "Well, Julia, I am happy to meet you."

The conversation suddenly seemed out of place. His

20

tone indicated something personal between them, as if he knew her from somewhere, and that she wouldn't be able to shake him off easily. When he then walked over to the hotel desk, she felt a wave of relief, and was glad that her idea had been wrong. But relief was short-lived. He returned and stood in front of her. At least he didn't presume too much familiarity by sitting down next to her.

"I ordered some Limca for us," he said.

"But really, that was quite unnecessary." She realized that he must have heard the whole of her conversation with Harry.

After a few minutes of silence a barefooted servant in white pants and a high-collared shirt-jacket came and deposited Limca bottles on the Formica-topped teapoy in front of them. Julia ignored the drink.

"Go on, drink it," coaxed Selvam.

She stiffly took the bottle. The wet coolness in her hand reminded her with an electriclike shock of the intense heat of the day and the additional heat which flushed through her body from Selvam's presence. She sipped from the straw.

Selvam's combination of aggressiveness and gentleness confused Julia. She couldn't distinguish between the knots of apprehension and the knots of interest tangled in her chest. But she wasn't so confused that she forgot her resolve. Long ago she had put Indian men completely off limits—the only sensible thing to do in a country of arranged caste marriages.

Julia finally spoke with a tinge of sarcasm. "I suppose you came back to get married and then you'll be off to the States again."

A smile spread slowly across his face. "I see you know much about India." He paused. "I'm sure my parents will

21

soon be making arrangements for my marriage. They wanted me to get married six years ago."

"And you didn't want to."

"I had no need for a wife."

She knew exactly what he meant—he didn't need a wife when plenty of girls were so easy. She gave him her look of chisled ice.

"Don't misunderstand." He must have guessed her thought. He looked very amused. "I was too busy studying to have anything to do with women, and then my job has been very demanding."

Smug, arrogant liar, pretending innocence, she thought, looking away from him. She couldn't believe a man as handsome as Selvam, who looked to be in his thirties, wouldn't have been involved with women. And he definitely wasn't shy, not by Indian standards or American either. But she wasn't sure that he was lying. His voice did sound sincere.

When she looked up at him again, he was looking down at her in a hard and serious manner. His eyes glided freely over her face and body. As an automatic reflex she pulled at the part of her sari covering her thin blouse. She pulled it up to her throat.

Very gently he asked, "Do you feel cold?"

The question struck Julia as personal, intimate even. He couldn't have meant for it to be taken literally, not in Tamil Nadu's hottest season. Her heart quickened and her face reddened. "No, of course not."

TWO

Julia thought the conversation had gone too far and felt relieved when the clerk came up to her.

"Your rooms are ready, miss."

A different barefooted servant stood just behind the clerk. Before Julia could stand up, he had lifted the two pieces of luggage, putting one on his head and the other in his hand. The clerk then gave him the key.

Julia followed the servant. She didn't look again at Selvam, but she could feel him staring at her as she left the lobby. It took all her strength to keep her knees from buckling. The enervating heat could have made her weak, and all the travel—five hours on the train—but she knew that Selvam had affected her strangely. She was glad to be rid of him.

Alone in the hotel room, Julia went into the bathroom and switched on the small hot-water heater clamped to the wall. Everything was there for a nice hot Indian bath, the large brass bucket and the aluminum cup for pouring water over her body.

Julia didn't use the shower spigot because it was aimed straight down and her hair would get wet. Anyway, her bathroom at home—at the clinic—didn't have a shower spigot and she had become used to the bucket bath.

After thoroughly washing off the layers of salt, dirt, and

coal dust she had accumulated from traveling all day, she dressed in a gray-and-white checked robe and lay down on the bed. Outside her window among the young coconut trees swayed a tree with brilliant red flowers, flowers that seemed to have been painted there by some artist with a palette knife and gypsy lipstick. She recalled the name, Flame of the Forest, and with that last vision she fell asleep.

The first knock on the door didn't wake her. It was absorbed into her dream. Then on the second knock she woke suddenly and felt a twist of fear in her chest. The next knocks were louder. Julia shook the sleep from her head.

"Is it Leela?" she called.

"Yes, Julia?"

Julia got up and opened the door. Leela and Raman entered and put the boxes they were carrying down in a corner near the teak almirah. Then Leela turned to Julia.

"You look different."

"When you knocked . . . well, I was sound asleep. I didn't know who it was." Julia's voice trembled slightly. "Here is the key to the other room." She took the key from the bedside table and handed it to Raman. How could she have thought it was that man Selvam?

"Let us eat early this night," suggested Raman. "Perhaps as soon as we are ready."

On the train they had eaten only some lemon rice packed in plantain leaves. They all agreed to have dinner at seven instead of the usual eight or nine. Then Raman went over to his room.

"Julia, why were you so different, so frightened?" asked Leela. Nothing escaped her. She always pried into each small issue, like a child opening mussels on a beach.

"It was really stupid of me," said Julia. "I shouldn't have stayed in the hotel lobby alone."

"What happened?"

"I didn't think a man would stare at me."

"Oh, that. But it happens to all young girls, especially pretty ones like you. Boys are becoming very bold these days. But do not be worried about those crazy boys. They are harmless."

"But he wasn't a typical crazy boy. I'm used to those. He was quite a bit older, in his thirties maybe. That's what disturbed me. Then he came and talked to me, well, in an improper manner, but I couldn't leave because of the luggage."

"*Che, che,* such a man. It is better I stayed here with you." Compassion spread over Leela's face.

Julia didn't tell her how his black hair fell across his forehead and how his voice had a deep gentleness. "Well, it's over and done with," said Julia with resolve, changing to a cheerful voice. "I'm going to be more careful from now on."

While Leela bathed, Julia let down her hair and brushed it until the dim light above the dressing table caught its shine. It had grown long and thick in two years, and fell almost to her waist. It would be out of style back in America, she thought a bit morosely, hating the idea of having to cut even one inch of it.

Julia took a long cotton dress out of her suitcase and changed into it—her own creation with the help of Mrs. Arokiaswamy's treadle sewing machine. It was made from a green, blue, and white floral print, and because it was sleeveless, would be quite refreshing in the heat. The V-neck was a little too low for India, but she'd be with American friends tonight.

Leela emerged from the bathroom in a clean sari blouse

and white cotton petticoat, gathered at her waist and hanging down to her ankles. "See the lovely girl!" she said noticing Julia's dress.

"Oh, I forgot to tell you. I'm meeting some Peace Corps friends after dinner," said Julia.

"So they were able to find you?"

"Yes. They came here when they didn't see me at the Lakshmi. Why don't you and Raman join us? There's going to be a band here tonight."

"Oh, no, we are old people. You enjoy with your friends." Leela took out a chiffon sari—a brown and white leaf print—from her suitcase and proceeded to wrap it around her, tucking it in, deftly making pleats with one hand while holding the rest of the fabric in the other, tucking some more, and finally draping the end over her left shoulder. She then leaned toward the mirror and applied a large red dot of *kungamam* powder to her forehead. "Julia, you will do something with your hair, is it not?"

"Yes, Mother," said Julia, stressing each syllable in mock complaint. They looked at each other and smiled. Julia took a blue barrette out of her cosmetic bag. She pulled back some hair from both sides and locked the barrette in back. That way her hair would not get in her face, and yet would fall freely down her back.

"That is better," said Leela, "though still very much style."

In a few minutes Raman came. The three of them went out for dinner and then a stroll. The streets were lighted by shops, neon lights, and the hurricane lanterns of sidewalk merchants. The new moon's silver crescent hung as an ornament in the sky rather than a source of light.

It was nearly eight o'clock when Julia parted company with Raman and Leela. Instead of going through the lobby, she crossed through the dark courtyard and entered the dining hall from a side door. The balmy breeze, pretending to cool the extreme heat, wafted in through the floor-length windows on the two long sides of the hall.

Harry and Jean were dancing to the electric guitar and saxophone music of the band. Julia found Rick at one of the tables and sat down with him.

Rick had been interested in Julia in the beginning, and she had been attracted to him. Though he had been quite delicate, his demands had proven too much for Julia, and she had rebuffed his advances. Her standoffish manner with men had made Aunt Frances long ago comment about how it would take a very persistent man to win her heart. Aunt Frances, of course, had no idea about the dishonorable intentions of men, since she had married just out of high school and then had devoted herself to her career.

Rick was basically a decent man, and honorable by modern standards—Julia had realized that later. He was not, however, persistent. Now he and Jean were engaged. Julia still liked him and felt comfortable with him.

"Doesn't this hotel make you think of the days when the British were here?" she asked.

Rick, slightly husky with a heavy jaw, stared at Julia and squeezed his brow. "How do you mean?"

"Well, it seems this must have been built by the British. Once we got a room with an old claw-footed bathtub, terribly eroded near the drain. Of course we didn't use it. It didn't even have a plug. But it struck me that this hotel was built by the British, especially for the British."

Rick looked around the dining room at places where the plaster had peeled off the walls, pillars, and high ceiling. "Well, it sure looks old enough. It is quite a dilapidated place."

"Maybe it's even more than a hundred years old. See that gray wooden floor in the middle? I bet that's where they danced when they held balls a century ago. You don't see many wooden floors in India."

"No, you don't," agreed Rick. "You sure are perceptive tonight." He smiled his handsome smile which had attracted Julia to him in the first place.

"And over on the stage where the band is, I'd guess they used to put the orchestra there. Can't you just hear a Strauss waltz and see the lords and ladies spinning around the dance floor, the ladies in heavily petticoated gowns of all colors . . . like so many spinning tops?"

"It's too much of a strain for my imagination, lady. I'm dead tired and the heat's so draining. All I see are a bunch of haggard tourists trying to disco."

"And these chairs we're sitting in," continued Julia, ignoring Rick's lack of interest in her imagined world, "they're at least a century old, straight from the Victorian era."

Rick rocked a little in his high, straight-backed chair to prove the point. "I frankly prefer modern, comfortable places like the Lakshmi. Maybe I'm just getting a little anxious to go home."

"But I'm not referring to physical conditions. Who doesn't like some comfort? It's this land I'm referring to. It's full of layers and worlds." Julia's eyes danced in the light and her smile became intense.

Rick looked puzzled.

"Like this British layer," continued Julia, "and there's the Dravidian-Tamil layer dating back before the Harappan civilization over four thousand years ago. You can see the influence in the village goddesses and the Indian preoccupation with bathing and purity. You know they had the most advanced sewer and drainage system in the

28

world at that time. They're still using that same type of system in many of the towns."

"Gee, you've been doing your homework," said Rick with his mocking smile.

"Didn't you read the books that were on the suggested reading list?"

"Not all of them." Rick saw the embarrassed look on Julia's face. "Go on, tell me more about these worlds and layers of yours."

"Well, then there's the Vedic-Aryan layer which is perhaps responsible for the overthrow of the Harappan civilization. It can be seen in scriptural Hinduism, in the paramount gods and goddesses. And the Mughal layer. Those Muslim conquerors ruled Northern India for almost a thousand years. I know they weren't here in the South for very long, but when I see a cluster of Muslim women all covered in white sheets—they look so different and yet they are just another part, another layer of India."

"Yes, I see what you mean," said Rick. "You could say there was a slightly different world of customs and beliefs for each caste, even, not to mention for each religious group—Hindu, Buddhist, Muslim, Christian."

"And there's the modern, jet-set layer." Julia laughed and her eyes sparkled. "Isn't it surprising, even thrilling, to see the modern and traditional side by side?"

Again Rick looked puzzled. Julia continued, "Like when you see a bullock cart in the tradition of thousands of years ago right alongside a modern bus."

"The buses are sort of ancient too," teased Rick.

Julia smiled. "I know what you mean." Then a gnawing pang of isolation focused her attention on yet two other worlds. "And there's the man's world and the woman's world."

"Well, I have no problems with that," said Rick. "I'm totally out of the woman's world."

"It's hard for me," said Julia, more to herself than to Rick. "I'm uncomfortable in the man's world, and I'm not really accepted in the woman's world, except at the clinic. Even though I could pass as an Indian—well, I *am* half Indian—you know how the women are, they don't accept you into their inner circle unless you're related."

"It's nothing to worry about now that we're going home." He turned his attention to the dancers. "Would you like to dance?"

"No, thanks," said Julia, then regretted it because she really did want to dance. But by that time Rick had left and was cutting in on Harry and Jean. Though a bit heavy, Rick was an excellent dancer and he reeled Jean in some fancy spins while Harry, looking dejected, came over to sit with Julia.

Bad mistake, she thought, hoping Harry wouldn't ask her to dance. The last time he had stepped all over her feet, and the first time he had tried to make a pass at her—she couldn't forget that because it had soured her relationship with him ever since.

Fortunately he didn't ask. Instead he sat down and looked ready to start up a conversation. But Julia didn't even want to talk to him. He would certainly spoil her reverie about her multilayered India. He simply lacked the finesse that Rick had.

Just as Julia was trying to figure out how to escape Harry, she felt a light touch on her shoulder, as if a hummingbird had perched there. She looked at the large, tan hand and followed it up the blue sleeve to Selvam's handsome face. He had shaved and his very black hair had been neatly combed. Quite a change from the grisly Mughal conqueror or rowdy Greek sailor images he had conjured up earlier that day. Still an imposing person, he looked more like a Chola king—stately and aggressive, rather than merely ruthless and aggressive.

"Come, let's dance," he said.

Because she was caught completely off guard, and because she wanted to escape Harry, she accepted. Selvam escorted her to the dance floor with remarkable grace. His gestures, the hint of a bow when he had spoken, made it seem as if he had been finely schooled in all the gentlemanly arts. She forgot about her earlier resolve to put him off with the cool aloofness of an Indian woman. Because he made her feel just now like a lady, she relaxed, and took the part.

Julia and Selvam danced to the quick tempo of the music. To her surprise, because most Indians frowned upon dancing, he was quite an expert. Julia had to strain just to keep her mind and body together so she could follow him. He taught her as they danced, but any observer would have thought they were long-term partners. While Julia tried to add nervous smiles now and then, juggling them with efforts in learning, Selvam remained as cool as rose milk and took every opportunity to survey her—her sleeveless arms and deep décolletage pointing to a hint of cleavage.

Just to wipe the satisfaction off his face, she asked with mock coquettishness, "So how did you learn to dance if you didn't have anything to do with girls?"

"You have a very good recollection of our conversation, Miss Julia. About dancing, I picked it up from the movies."

Julia raised her brow in disbelief.

"All right, there were a few girls, but I just danced with them. I like dancing very much." He seemed to be embarrassed by the admission.

In India chastity was almost as much a virtue for men as it was for women. Apparently Selvam wasn't sure if Julia's attitude would be Indian or Western concerning the male-female relationship.

Julia said with great amusement, "Don't worry, I won't tell your father."

A smile spread over Selvam's face, but he didn't say anything. The band changed to a slow dance, and Julia indicated she was tired and wanted to sit down, but Selvam pulled her into his arms with such force that her breath was squeezed from her. Retaliation, she thought, for her taunt. She struggled, but he held her locked tightly. Because she didn't want to cause a scene, she simply scolded herself for ever having accepted his invitation to dance.

Slowly he relaxed his grip as they moved with the rhythm of the music, and she, too, relaxed. His hard body pressing lightly now against her soft curves stirred up sensations she didn't want to acknowledge. He pushed her head to his shoulder with his hand, while Julia's heart pounded. She warned herself not to get carried away.

By the middle of the dance he had maneuvered her to a door, and then out into the dark courtyard. The scent of jasmine and honeysuckle greeted them and the sliver of new moon winked from above. Selvam reached up and picked a sprig of jasmine blossoms and leaves from a creeper.

"You're not wearing flowers tonight," he said. "Let me put this in your hair."

Julia's pulse quickened at the gentleness of Selvam's words. Quelling any rational objections, she turned and let him place the flowers just above the barrette. His touch lingered on her hair, and then he grasped her hand and turned her back to him. Before Julia could protest, he brought her hand to his lips. He held it there for a long time, and just that single point of contact, his warm lips pressed against her hand, sent waves of heat through her body. It felt more sensuous than any kiss she had ever experienced.

Julia had always felt threatened by or unprepared for kisses she had received on dates. But this simple kissing of her hand enticed without threatening. She fell into a trance, into a world apart from reality, a world which contained only her and Selvam.

It seemed to Julia that Selvam was a gentle prince in a happily-ever-after world, and she didn't want anything to happen to break the spell. She didn't want to get more involved—which could only lead nowhere—but she didn't want him to stop kissing her hand either. Her breathing became slightly erratic as he explored her palm with his lips.

If only life could remain suspended like this forever, she thought, a sleeping-beauty spell to be cast at this moment. Keats's image of figures on a Grecian urn suddenly became meaningful to her, and she thought of the lines:

> Bold Lover, never, never canst thou kiss
> Though winning near the goal—yet, do not grieve:
> She cannot fade, though thou hast not thy bliss,
> For ever wilt thou love, and she be fair!

"I wish life could be like that," she whispered to herself.

Selvam pressed her hand to his hot cheek, which gave her the simultaneous sensations of smooth skin, fine emery cloth of a recently shaved beard, and muscles tensing underneath. "How?" he asked.

"Huh? Oh, like in 'Ode on a Grecian Urn.' A silly thought." She felt embarrassed by her sentimentality. But then he probably wouldn't know what she meant. Most educated Indians were only interested in science and technology, Julia had concluded.

Much to her surprise and delight he quoted the first line, "Thou still unravish'd bride of quietness . . ."

He pulled her to him and they danced in the darkness, surrounded by the sweet perfume of jasmine and honeysuckle. He stroked her back, not with the desire pent up by a lifetime of celibacy, but with the skill of one who has had much practice. He knew just how to hold her to create in her a growing desire without creating fear.

The music ended, but Selvam continued to hold Julia firmly in his arms, brushing his cheek against her forehead. She didn't want it to end. They stood without music, his arms locked around her.

Finally, after some faster music started, he released her, keeping one of her hands in his.

"Well," he said and inhaled deeply. "I'd like to take you for a drink, but since Tamil Nadu's dry, let's go instead for some ice cream at the Imperial. It's so wretchedly hot."

The Imperial was the best place in town for ice cream, but it was quite far, beyond walking distance. She searched for an excuse, and said feebly, "I don't know, my mother . . . I mean, my friend . . ."

"Your mother?" Selvam raised his eyebrows and smiled at her. "Do Peace Corps workers bring their mothers with them?"

"No, of course not. I meant the lady I'm with—she's like a mother to me, sort of strict and protective. She'd be worried. . . ."

"What's there to worry about? I'll bring you back in one piece. I'm not some sort of monster."

Julia wasn't sure about that. So far her impressions of

Selvam ran the gamut from gentleman to rogue. "I don't really think . . ." she said weakly.

Without further hesitation Selvam led her through the courtyard to the arch of the hotel driveway. "Come on, *ma.*" Julia started at his use of *ma* from the Tamil word, *amma.* It meant mother, but was used as a term of endearment, especially for young girls in a very close relationship. He was becoming too openly familiar. "We need something to cool us," he said. "I'd forgotten how hot India is during this season."

"If you promise we'll return soon," said Julia. She still hesitated, though she felt relatively safe in public.

He didn't reply. He was busy hailing down a cycle rickshaw. A young rickshaw man in a sleeveless undershirt and khaki shorts cycled up to them. Selvam bargained with him in Tamil and they climbed in. Because of the small size of the seat, Selvam's left side—his arm, hip, and leg—pressed firmly against Julia's right side.

Julia was glad the hood was down. She felt the increasing coolness as the rickshaw started moving, slowly at first, under the force of the rickshaw man's weight on the pedals. The muscles on his back rippled with the initial strain, but soon they were going fast with ease, coasting at times.

"Is she your girl friend?" asked the man in Tamil, turning his head to Selvam's side.

"*En manaivi,*" said Selvam.

Julia's heart jumped. *En manaivi,* my wife. He had called her his wife. Then she thought, but of course, it would be the only thing he could say to avoid embarrassment. Dating and girl friends were strictly taboo, at least for most Indians.

The rickshaw man continued to ask questions. Selvam explained to him how he—he and his wife—had just

35

arrived from America. The rickshaw man, in a very joyous mood, probed and asked more questions. Then he offered information about himself.

Julia understood Tamil and learned that he had two wives and had to work very hard to support them, although one worked in a factory and that helped out. He did know it was now illegal to have two wives, but the first one couldn't have children. Now he had a son by his second wife. He looked about twenty-five or twenty-six, a fine athletic build.

The driver flexed his muscles as he cycled up the slight incline of the bridge over the Coovam River. Streetlights and shop lights glistened on the water like dancing girls in sequined costumes. Julia was next to Selvam, the most handsome man she had ever met, his warm arm and leg touching her. Again Julia wished time could stand still at this very moment of exquisite beauty and emotion. Then, past the crest of the bridge, they quickly coasted down the other side.

After a few more streets and a few more turns, the rickshaw made a U-turn and pulled up in front of the Imperial Hotel. The coolness of the air-conditioned room, as they entered the hotel, seemed to Julia like a reprieve from the oven heat of Madras. Selvam led her over the thick, red carpeting to a small table in the corner of the nearly empty dining room.

Julia wanted to know more about Selvam, where he lived, and what his occupation was—things she wouldn't have asked in the rickshaw after he had said they were married, since the rickshaw man undoubtedly knew some English.

Those words, *en manaivi,* intrigued her. Perhaps Selvam was open to marrying outside his caste. She wanted to know that, too—not that she was interested in marriage, she told herself. She just wanted to find out about him. And she wanted to tell him about herself, that her mother was Indian.

The waiter appeared with menus. He looked much more dignified than the servers at the Queen's Palace in his white European-style jacket, black pants, bow tie, and shining black shoes. He even looked more dignified than the guests at the Queen's Palace. Julia supposed that they didn't serve just anyone who walked in off the street, but then only moneyed people would come to a place like this.

The prices on the menu startled Julia. For the cost of a special ice cream dish one could buy a complete meal at other restaurants. She chose a dish of plain vanilla ice cream, the cheapest item on the menu.

Selvam looked at her sharply and said, "You don't have to watch your weight." He reordered the most expensive item for both of them, the Honeymoon Special.

When the waiter left, Julia asked pointedly, "Why did you say I was your wife to the rickshaw man?"

Selvam raised his brow. "So, you understand Tamil."

"I should say so! After working in a village for two years."

He wasn't going to answer her question directly. "That driver was too nosy. He talked too much."

Julia felt surprised to hear Selvam complain after the very open way they had conversed. "I sort of like him," she said. "He's so friendly. He seems like such an interesting man, young and attractive, not like other rickshaw men."

A flash of dark emotion crossed Selvam's face, making him even more handsome, though formidable. "Then maybe you could become his third wife!" His cutting voice surprised Julia. It had always been so gentle. But then she had only known him for a few hours.

Julia pressed her lips together and glared at him. "Ever since we met, you've acted like you own me or something, staring at me the way you did. It is really none of your business whom I marry. But, in any case, you don't have to insult me by suggesting that I become the third wife of some man!"

"I was staring at you?" Selvam picked up on the minor accusation. "You were staring at me, my dear, with those compelling eyes. What do you expect a man like myself to do, ignore it?"

The waiter came with their ice cream, interrupting their argument before Julia could explain that she had been looking at the statue of Our Lady and not at Selvam. They ate their Honeymoon Specials in silence. The moment for explanations had passed.

After they finished, Selvam pulled out a cigarette and smoked, taking long drags. While he looked past her, staring blankly into the distance, Julia studied his face, the strong jawline, rigidly set now, and the shadow of a beard already appearing only a few hours after he had shaved. His slightly aquiline nose and leaf-shaped eyes were so very characteristically Tamil.

Selvam crushed out his cigarette, then focused his gaze on Julia. Her heart skipped. He didn't say anything, but simply moved his head, indicating they should leave.

Back on the street, Julia rubbed her bare arms. The heat outside actually felt good after being in the very cold restaurant. Selvam looked for another rickshaw or taxi, but Julia quickly climbed into the one they had come in. Since there were no others in sight, Selvam climbed in too.

The rickshaw started back to the Queen's Palace and the rickshaw man, in his glorious, joyous mood, started singing a song from a Tamil movie. He had an excellent baritone voice.

Julia still felt upset about what Selvam had said, yet she enjoyed the feel of his arm and leg against her, the hardness of his muscles which sent electrical pulses through her body. Then he covered the back of her hand with his hand. It felt warm, giving her a pleasant jolt.

"I'm a jealous man," he said very quietly. "That's how I am."

Julia relaxed and patted his hand lightly with her other hand. "I didn't expect you to be so jealous."

"Neither did I," he whispered, then raised his voice and spoke in Tamil to the rickshaw man, "Could you take us around the city for some time?"

The rickshaw man stopped singing long enough to agree and then started another song.

They left the main business streets and drove through residential areas where the houses were like rows of apartments, all adjacent to each other. Old men and young men were seated or sleeping out on some of the small, pillared verandas. At one house a woman was bringing a tray of refreshments to the men. Then the rickshaw had to squeeze by a small crowd and a makeshift structure of bamboo poles and palm thatch, protruding from a house. It was a marriage *pandal.* Julia peered in and saw the bride dressed in a white cotton sari and the groom in a white, ankle-length *dhoti* with a thin gold border.

"They're wearing *maru* clothes," Selvam explained. "They would have been married this morning in wedding clothes provided by the groom's side, and now they've changed into clothes the bride's side has given."

They rode around on other streets and saw several marriage *pandals,* most of them deserted now.

"So many marriages all on one day," said Julia.

"It must be an auspicious day according to the astrologers," replied Selvam, "aside from it being the marriage season, the phase of the waxing moon, and a Friday—Mondays, Wednesdays, and Fridays are good for marriages." Then he asked the rickshaw man, who replied that it was indeed an auspicious day, that his second wife's sister had also been married that morning.

"A very auspicious day," repeated Selvam to Julia, and gently squeezed her hand.

Julia blushed at the thought that the young, shy brides would now be on their flower-strewn marriage beds with their young and equally shy bridegrooms.

At the Queen's Palace Hotel, Selvam gave a very generous tip to the rickshaw man and told him to buy something for his son. Alone, Selvam and Julia walked hand in hand to the archway of the hotel. To the left was the lobby and to the right, a flight of stairs leading to Julia's room. The sliver of new moon had disappeared from the sky.

"We have many things to talk about," said Selvam.

Julia wanted very much to stay and hear what he had to say, but instead she released her hand and started to back away from him. "It's getting late and my friend will be worried."

"Wait." He grabbed her hand back and held it firmly. "I thought you would come with me . . ."

"Where?" She looked at him, widening her soft brown eyes. It wasn't what he had said as much as the way he had said it—hesitatingly, in a voice heavy with portent.

Then he stated in a flat tone, ". . . to my room."

The vision of his dark room made Julia wince. It took a while for her to realize exactly what he meant. It was so sudden, so unexpected. But when she did understand the implications, her whole body shook with anger. "For what!" she demanded, more for a final verification of his impudence than to find out what he had meant.

His smile mocked her. "You look so beautiful when

you're angry. Did anyone ever tell you that?" He kept her hand tightly in his.

"Answer me!" She raised her voice as much as she dared in public.

"No, you answer me." He shifted to a serious mood. "Did anyone ever tell you how beautiful you are?" She glared at him, not about to answer his question, until he said roughly, "Never mind. Now I asked you to come to my room. Surely you're not so innocent that you don't know what for."

"Oh! You—you!" she stammered. His tone of voice was so insulting, his request so blatant. Most men would have at least tried to make it sound romantic. But then Selvam was on his way to get married—or so he had indicated earlier—pausing only for a quick interlude with Julia. She should have stuck with her initial impression of him. Instead she had let herself in for his insult.

Gritting her teeth, Julia shook her hand loose from Selvam's. She whirled away and the sprig of jasmine blossoms he had put in her hair fell to the ground.

As she ran up the stairs, he called out to her, "Next time you won't run away from me, Julia."

At the hotel room Julia pounded on the door. In a few seconds Leela opened it.

"Julia, you look sick. Come in, *ma.*" Leela wrinkled her brow.

"Oh, it's . . . it's just a headache." For the first time Julia wished they didn't have this protective attitude toward young women. She wished Leela would go sleep in her husband's room, so she could be alone to simmer in her anger. And yet she was glad Leela was with her. She felt afraid—afraid, angry, and confused.

Never, never again, she vowed silently as she lay on her bed a few minutes later, not even for a moment would she

41

ever allow a man to insult or trick her. She would go back to Little Bear, Wisconsin, where she had lived before her aunt and uncle had taken her to Milwaukee. There was a small hospital, not much larger than the Tamaraiyur clinic. She would be a nurse there.

Her mind jumped to the future. She pictured herself as a middle-aged spinster saying with melancholy to the young nurses, "I guess chivalry is dead." She laughed inwardly at that ridiculous image. Then she became serious as her mind returned to Selvam, to his strong face, dark, leaf-shaped eyes, alluring lips, and black, black hair . . . and he had quoted Keats. "Thou still unravish'd bride of quietness," he had said with such gentleness, such feeling, as if he were speaking of her.

Selvam had points about him, not just good looks, which attracted her enormously. It even seemed that they were meant for each other. And then he had spoiled everything. She could have really fallen in love with someone like Selvam. It would have been so easy. She gasped at that last thought, almost awakening Leela. She thanked God that she had not been enraptured by him to the extent of going to his room.

THREE

Julia walked quickly up the road through the Tamaraiyur clinic compound. Her maroon-and-orange print wrap-around skirt fluttered in the early morning breeze. She, Leela, and Raman had returned from Madras late the previous night, after spending Saturday shopping—the joy of it lost for Julia.

Selvam's words, *Next time you won't run away from me,* kept haunting her. At first, angered by his suggestion that she go to his room, she had thought indignantly, *There won't be a next time!* But now the words came back as a growing threat. It occurred to her that Raman would have written her name and clinic address in the hotel registry. With a little artful bribery, Selvam could easily find out where she lived.

The clinic looked so peaceful at this early morning hour. The sun, like a flame flickering between distant coconut trees, threw an orange glow on the clinic buildings. It seemed impossible that anything could threaten this world which had become her world. And yet, if a strange man were to show up and create a scene by pursuing her and insulting her, she would suddenly fall from grace. Gossip, condescending glances, perhaps even some rudely suggestive remarks would all be foisted upon her.

43

What was the Tamil saying? It takes years to build up a reputation, but only a minute for people to say *che*.

Julia did realize how unlikely it was for a man, even one as audacious as Selvam, to seek her out at the village clinic, but she always suffered from overimagination, as her aunt had diagnosed it, conjuring up negative visions, as well as positive. And she often lost precious moments of sleep in the process.

She didn't stop at the student residence-commissary building across from the duplex that she shared with Leela and Raman. With more than an hour before mass, Rita and Susheela, the two Catholic student nurses, would still be sleeping. Julia had awakened early, but she didn't want to rob those women of a few more minutes of sleep.

Julia walked out of the clinic compound and headed for Dr. Arokiaswamy's house, a large two-story structure a quarter of a mile away, but visible from the clinic. The stonework staircase housing rose up three stories to the top of the flat roof, and gave it the look of a formal mansion. But its off-pink color—reminding Julia of the color she used to create as a child by mixing up the chocolate, strawberry, and vanilla in Neapolitan ice cream—gave it an inviting warmth.

As she crossed under the trellised arcade of magenta bougainvillea into the garden of exotic flowers and tropical trees, she caught sight of Mrs. Arokiaswamy, her plump, still youthful figure bent over at the foot of the expansive veranda. She was making a *kolam*, a complex design of rice flour lines curved in and out among dots. It was supposed to keep away *Peeda*, the demon of laziness.

"*Vanga, vanga,*" greeted Mrs. Arokiaswamy with her gracious smile. At forty-five she had only a trace of gray in her black hair. The large, red *kungamam* dot made her round face seem even rounder.

44

"Vanakkam," responded Julia, pressing the palms of her hands together.

In Tamil Mrs. Arokiaswamy said, "Arul informed us you came late last night." Arul, the clinic's driver and maintenance man, had picked them up at the railway station. "Please go in and have some coffee. We will be going to mass in the jeep." She smiled much more than usual. Her whole face glowed.

"Why are you so happy today?" asked Julia in her broken Tamil.

"My son, Joseph, came home yesterday morning."

"Oh, he did? Then Leela was right. She said he would come soon."

They spoke for a few more minutes. Though Julia could understand Tamil, she had some difficulty speaking it. Finally Julia slipped off her sandals on the veranda near the wooden plank swing and stepped inside onto the cool tiles of polished green marble chip mosaic. The main hall had very little furniture for its huge size, two teak and cane settees, a few rosewood armchairs, and a French provincial sofa, plus an assortment of cabinets and small tables.

The room would have appeared austere from its immense size and high ceiling, but instead it felt homy because of the walls. They were cluttered with pictures—religious ones of the saints and Jesus, one of a guardian angel spreading wings over a small boy and girl —calendars also with religious pictures, and family portraits and photographs of various sizes. In an ornate niche on the far wall, as if presiding over the room, were statues of Mary, Jesus, and Joseph. Chains of jasmine flowers had been placed at their feet.

As Julia glanced around the room, she noticed a change. On a portrait of a young woman someone had hung a thick jasmine garland on top of the permanent garland of curled sandalwood shavings. She had never really paid much attention to the portrait before. The woman in it was quite beautiful. Her black hair, dark eyes, and the red dot on her forehead contrasted with her olive complexion. Julia wondered who it was. It didn't look like Nirmala or Mrs. Arokiaswamy.

"Julia." Nirmala stood brimming with joy. She was tall for a Tamil girl, five feet and four inches, the same height as Julia, but a little too slender, a factor which had caused some gossip among the clinic staff about how much dowry Dr. Arokiaswamy would have to give. "Please sit down," she said. "Tetru is making coffee."

"I heard a car this morning. Did Dr. Arokiaswamy go on an emergency call?" asked Julia.

"No, that was my brother. He returned yesterday. This morning he went for his friend's wedding in Chidambaram."

"On Sunday?"

"Yes. The ceremonies start tonight, then the wedding will be tomorrow."

"So, your brother returned," said Julia to make conversation.

"Yes. It was such a surprise. I knew he would come. *Appa* was really the one surprised: He had tears in his eyes and they embraced each other." While Nirmala spoke, Julia imagined the touching scene of Dr. Arokiaswamy embracing his son. "Then we all got tears, even Joe *annan*."

The servant, Tetru, a middle-aged woman in a green cotton sari, brought in the coffee and left it on the table.

Julia's mind drifted away from Nirmala's talk about her brother. She brooded to herself about how Selvam had insulted her. She had not failed to detect the note of derision in his voice when he had asked her to go to his room.

Mrs. Arokiaswamy entered and saw the coffee on the table. "You did not drink your coffee," she said in Tamil.

Julia answered, "Not hungry. Stomach ache." Knowing that refusing food was a sign of aloofness, she managed to take a few sips.

"It was all so grand," said Nirmala, "two weeks before my wedding. *Annan* brought two large suitcases full of presentations for me."

Such an insult, thought Julia. Even in America it was an insult to some extent, to be so blatant as Selvam had been. Here it was . . . she couldn't think of a strong enough word.

"He has really changed," continued Nirmala. "*Amma* said, 'He left as a boy and returned as a man.' *Appa* told him that if he had the habit of smoking, he could smoke in his presence. Then Joe *annan* smoked his American cigarette. Did you see, he brought this sari back for me."

Julia came back to the reality of the moment. "That's very nice." Nirmala wore a red nylon sari with a white flower print, more flowers at the bottom to give the effect of a border. "The flowers look like jasmine."

"Yes, that is just what *annan* said. He brought back so many things for my wedding, he had to pay over one thousand rupees at customs."

"Your brother is very thoughtful, very generous. Is he going to stay in India?"

"He said he might. *Appa* was even more surprised and overjoyed."

Julia knew through clinic gossip that there had been some kind of strained relation between Dr. Arokiaswamy and his son, which would explain why the doctor had been surprised. She couldn't, however, understand how anyone could have problems with Dr. Arokiaswamy. He was the most dedicated, self-sacrificing person she knew. Every-

47

one respected him. He was an excellent surgeon, who could have become famous elsewhere, and yet he served the village people. His government salary was substantial, and he was independently wealthy, but he could have easily doubled his fortune as a big city doctor. Julia doubted that Joseph would ever measure up to Dr. Arokiaswamy, despite all the praise Leela had given him.

"And then of course we spoke about Rita," said Nirmala with an aura of smugness. "There was quite a fuss about her."

Julia braced herself mentally for Nirmala's outpouring of gossip against her cousin Rita which would certainly follow. She found it difficult to believe that Nirmala was her age, had a master's degree in Tamil literature, and would be married soon. Her jealousy of Rita seemed so childish.

Rita had come to the clinic a year ago as a nursing student in Julia's health care program. Her father had died when she was a baby and her mother had long since gone through the family wealth, but Rita never seemed to envy Nirmala's wealth and education. She was slightly fairer than Nirmala, robust and earthy, willing to work hard. At nineteen she was much more mature than Nirmala and would make a good nurse or a good housewife, or both.

The problem between Nirmala and Rita had started three months ago when a family had come to "see" Nirmala with the idea of arranging marriage for their son. Rita was at the house that day, and when the boy's party found out she was a relative, and hence in the same caste, they turned their attention to her, much to Nirmala's chagrin. Nothing came of it, however. They decided against Nirmala, apparently because she was not beautiful enough, and also against Rita, because she was not wealthy enough.

Since then Nirmala had been jealous of Rita. It upset Julia because she liked them both. She felt bad about what Nirmala said next.

"Joe *annan* just stood right there. He is very tall." The sound of Mrs. Arokiaswamy in the dining room made Nirmala lower her voice, though it wasn't necessary because Mrs. Arokiaswamy didn't know English well. "He said that he refused to have his marriage arranged with Rita. *Appa* was angry. He demanded to know why. Then Joe *annan* said he was against cousin marriages. You may know, Julia, that in Tamil Nadu it is good for a boy to marry his mother's brother's daughter. He doesn't have to, but if they are the right age, it is thought to be good."

"What did your father say?" asked Julia.

"*Appa* put up much opposition. He said that was not a good reason and that since Joe *annan* had not married yet, for the last year *appa* and *amma* had been planning for him to marry Rita, ever since she came to the clinic."

"What did your brother say?"

"He became very angry and said it was because Rita did not have an education. He told them he would marry any girl they chose, but she must have at least a master's degree, that he would certainly prefer to marry a lady doctor, if one could be found in our caste. He didn't want Rita because she is poor, and he wanted at least fifty thousand rupees dowry and fifty sovereigns of gold for his wife's jewels."

Julia blinked at hearing about such greed, though she knew it was the custom. Dr. Arokiaswamy had fixed the same amount for Nirmala, and she was only marrying an engineer with a master of science. A medical doctor could easily get much more, especially one educated in America. "Then what did your father say to that?"

"What could *appa* say? Joe *annan* talks like a big man

49

now. *Appa* was upset and sad, but *annan* won the argument and *appa* had to go over to *annan*'s side. *Annan*'s reasons are very good ones. No one would deny that."

Julia raised her eyebrows and sighed. It would have been wonderful for Rita to marry Joseph. With her two gold bangles, chain, and loop earrings totaling about six sovereigns, and no money for a dowry, she didn't stand much chance to marry a well-educated man with a promising career.

"I sided with Joe *annan,*" said Nirmala. "I coaxed *amma* by telling her that *annan* should not marry someone so closely related, otherwise there might be trouble with the relatives."

"Nirmala!" shouted her mother in Tamil. "What are you talking in there? Guard your tongue. When you get married you should not carry any tales from this family to your husband's family. Do you understand?" Julia was surprised to find out that Mrs. Arokiaswamy knew more English than she had previously thought.

"Yes, *amma,*" Nirmala called back, then lowered her voice. "I told *amma* that I had some school chums of our own caste, Catholic, fair, and that we could arrange one of them for Joe *annan. Amma* told that she only wanted a good daughter-in-law who would be like a daughter to her. But then *appa* said we must drop the matter of Joe *annan*'s marriage until mine is over. Only then should we start to see girls for *annan.*"

Julia became bored by this gossip. It was unusual for a Tamil girl to be so open about her own family, but Julia suspected that Nirmala intended for her to spread the gossip to Rita, about what Rita's *athan,* Joseph, had said—*athan* meaning both elder cross cousin and husband. It would certainly be a blow to Rita, if she had been hoping for the match.

Just then Rita and Susheela entered the house dressed in their best nylon saris. And then Dr. Arokiaswamy came from upstairs, his thick white hair neatly combed. He was tall and lean, with a very light complexion. Except for his slightly stooped shoulders, making him look as if he had been carrying a heavy burden, he would appear the strong, old patriarch. His soft voice also contrasted with that image.

"Good morning, *vanakkam*. Everyone is ready?" he asked.

The five women and Dr. Arokiaswamy piled into the jeep outside and went three miles away to the village of Tamaraiyur, to a small church built by the Portuguese in the seventeenth century.

After mass, Julia changed into her nurse's uniform and went to work at the clinic, relieving Leela from duty. All of the twenty beds were occupied. The dry season brought more illness, mainly due to the poor quality of the drinking water. She made her rounds of the patients, checking their temperature, blood pressure, and other vital signs particular to each patient's condition.

Later in the afternoon Julia left the station to the other nurses and went and scrubbed down the surgical theater, disinfecting every inch of it. When she had first come, a servant woman had been in charge of cleaning it. Julia had been quick to notice that the woman did not have a good conception of the germ theory, and was not thorough. Since then Julia had taken over the job and had trained her nursing students. As a result staph infections had greatly decreased.

As she finished, Rita entered, dressed in the lavender sari she had worn to church. She called in a husky, feminine voice, "Julia."

"Oh, Rita, I thought Lata was working the night shift."

"Yes, I just wanted to talk to you."

Rita was generally frank and outspoken. She seemed shy today, but her black eyes glittered.

"About what?" asked Julia sweetly.

"About marriage."

"Well, I don't know if I can help you in that area since I'm not married myself." She smiled at Rita.

"I'm a little frightened," said Rita.

"You're strong and sensible. I've never known you to be frightened. Besides, you have plenty of time before you have to start thinking about marriage. You're only nineteen."

"But I will be married very soon."

"You didn't tell me. Has it been arranged for you?" Julia knitted her brows, suddenly worried about Rita.

"Since Joe *athan* came back from America it will be arranged very soon."

Julia's expression changed to shock. She remembered what Nirmala had said that morning, that Joseph didn't want to marry Rita. And here was Rita, thinking that Joseph would marry her, shimmering with happiness about it. Julia didn't know what to say. Perhaps Joseph would marry her in the end. If so, it would be better not to let Rita know what he had said to his family. Julia started cautiously, "Did you see Joseph when he returned?"

"Yes, of course. They called for me as soon as he came. He was angry when he learned I was staying in the students' hostel rather than with his parents. I had to explain that I wanted to be with the other girls and it was part of my training."

"What else did he tell you?"

"He said he would take care of everything, so that I will

be married very soon. I'm so happy and such a lucky girl. Joe *athan* is a very good man."

Rita seemed to be echoing what Leela had said about how good Joseph was, only now Julia had developed a bad impression of him. Not only did he refuse, behind her back, to marry Rita, but he seemed to be leading her on, making her think he would marry her.

"Why do you look so worried?" asked Rita.

"Oh, it's nothing. It's just taking me by surprise, your getting married so soon. Perhaps you shouldn't rush into it."

"But I have been planning on it for a long time. I knew from an early age who I would marry."

"Oh, Rita." Tears came to Julia's eyes as she thought about how Rita had been planning to marry her Joseph *athan* all these years. She put her hands on Rita's shoulders.

"Do not cry. I am the luckiest girl in the world."

Julia thought of Rita's happiness—the happiness of a girl in love—an experience Julia had never known. She thought of this happiness being crushed by the self-centered, cruel Joseph, whom she hadn't even met yet, and didn't care to meet. She embraced Rita.

"I'm not crying because I'm sad," she lied. "I'm crying because I'm so happy for you. I'm afraid I haven't been much help."

She controlled her tears and released Rita. "Whatever happens in your life, Rita, you know I'm your friend. I'll help you in any way I can. Now, it's getting late. Where's Lata? She should have come by now. You go and make Lata hurry up. I'm having dinner at Dr. Arokiaswamy's house tonight."

Rita left and in a few minutes Lata came and relieved Julia from duty. After an unheated bucket bath—the water in the area was never very cold—Julia changed into a silk sari of cream and violet Madras plaid. She had only two silk saris, the peacock blue one she had worn to Madras and the plaid one, but then she rarely had the opportunity to wear them. They made her look elegant and shapely, and she felt graceful as she walked over to Dr. Arokiaswamy's house.

Once there, however, Julia lost all sense of gracefulness. At formal dinner parties like this she felt out of place. Except for Mrs. Arokiaswamy, Nirmala, and herself, no women were present. Men usually didn't bring their wives to dinners and gatherings with non-relatives. Such dinners were in fact quite rare. Dr. Arokiaswamy and the other doctors in the area, however, frequently held these parties to discuss medical problems, schedules for surgery when several doctors were required to assist, and information on new treatments, procedures, and medicines. They invited Julia, the only nurse to attend, out of their sense of hospitality to a visitor in their land. Despite her Indian heritage, she was still an American to them.

Mrs. Arokiaswamy served refreshments in the main hall. Nirmala came for brief and polite greetings, then retreated. Julia sat uneasily in a rattan chair which had been brought in to help accommodate the guests. She stayed only a few minutes, contributing very little to the conversation. Then after drinking her lemonade and eating the fried appetizer and the sweet Mrs. Arokiaswamy had passed around, she arose and walked through the dining room.

The ten-foot-long dining table was neatly set with a white tablecloth, stainless steel plates and tumblers, and two centerpieces of wood roses. They were flowers that looked as if they had been carved from balsa wood. They

54

never failed to make Julia pause and appreciate their amazing deceptive appearance.

Instead of going directly out to the back veranda, Julia made a detour through the large kitchen and greeted Tetru and the other servants, who were busily adding last minute spices to the meal. Then she proceeded to the veranda and sat down at the small table with Nirmala. The red-and-white checkered print of the vinyl tablecloth, the soft glow from the veranda light, and the darkness surrounding them created a cozy atmosphere. In the courtyard past the veranda the raggedy leaves of the plantain trees, barely visible against the ink sky, seemed to be gossiping among themselves as they nodded in the breeze.

Nirmala smiled. "It is good you came tonight. I always feel lonely when *appa* has the doctors for dinner."

Julia suddenly realized that Nirmala perhaps felt more out of place than she. "It must be lonely for you here at the clinic." Since Nirmala had been away at college most of the time, and because of her split with Rita, she didn't have any friends nearby.

"It is so beautiful and peaceful here, but I do miss my school chums," replied Nirmala. "Madurai is a very nice city, but then I will terribly miss *amma* and *appa* when I go there." Julia felt it was fortunate that Nirmala's husband-to-be worked in Madurai where she had attended college. Leaving home wouldn't be such a jolting transformation for her. "And do you not feel lonely at times?" asked Nirmala.

"I love it here." Julia's eyes glittered. "I was a small-town girl and I never liked living in Milwaukee after my parents died. Cities are exciting to visit"—a trace of disgust crossed her face as she remembered her recent trip to Madras—"but I think this is paradise."

"Perhaps when you get married, you and your husband

can visit India and stay here with my family for some time."

Julia laughed. "It isn't that easy to get married in America. First a woman must find Mr. Right, and I have no intention to waste my time man hunting."

"You do not wish to get married?"

"I'm not against marriage, but it just isn't for me, at least not now. I don't seem to have any luck with men." She sighed, thinking about her brief escapade with Selvam.

Tetru came and set the table. Julia and Nirmala became silent as the noise of the doctors sitting down in the dining room echoed out onto the veranda, aware that they would be heard inside the house if they continued to speak.

Julia looked wistfully at her reflection in the large metal plate in front of her and wondered what it would be like to eat in the dining room with only family members. The table would not have the white tablecloth. The steel plates and dishes would be set directly on the woodlike Formica top. Formica. In India people considered Formica a luxurious addition to a teakwood table. That would be something to tell Aunt Frances, she thought.

Continuing her imaginary dinner, she guessed that Dr. Arokiaswamy would be at the head of the table. Joseph, his returned prodigal son, would be next to him, and then Nirmala. Mrs. Arokiaswamy would serve the meal and probably sit down to eat when the men were just about finished. It had something to do with rules of purity and pollution. Once a person had started eating he could not serve himself or others, so the server—usually the lady of the house—would eat last.

Dress would be informal, men in wrap-around *dhotis* or *kailis* and undershirts, women in cotton house saris. Conversation would be relaxed with an underlying tone of familiarity and strong family ties. Dr. Arokiaswamy would not be the formal type when it came to his family. Important topics would be interspersed with minor ones and joking. Perhaps Nirmala and Joseph would playfully fight over the last piece of mango, if Joseph were the playful type.

Julia smiled at the sudden realization that in order to be party to such a family meal she would have to be a family member, perhaps married to Joseph, as Leela had suggested. The fantasy faded with that thought.

While Tetru served them and they ate, the men in the dining room discussed medicine, the arrival of Dr. Arokiaswamy's son, the rising price of gold, and the difficulty of obtaining cement. The conversation had started out in English but had soon drifted into Tamil. Julia could understand most of it, but sometimes lost track of what they were saying.

All of a sudden she thought she heard the name Selvam or Selvanathan and a blush spread across her face. Of course it was a common name, not unusual, she told herself. She listened more keenly, trying to find out in what context the name had been used, but the topic shifted to problems with electricity cuts during these dry months.

Why, she asked herself, did she have to feel so embarrassed when she heard that name? No one knew what had happened. She hadn't even told Leela. And nothing like that would ever happen again, she swore, never.

She soon heard the name again—Dr. Selvanathan. She wasn't familiar with any Dr. Selvanathan, and she knew all the doctors in the area.

"I am sure Dr. Selvanathan will be a great help at your clinic," said one man. "He will allow you some rest, hmm, Dr. Arokiaswamy?"

"Yes. He is a fine doctor. Graduate of the University of

57

California Medical School," said Dr. Arokiaswamy. Everyone made sounds of approval. "I am very proud of him."

Julia thought they must be speaking about Dr. Arokiaswamy's son. According to the Tamil system of naming, the father's last name became a person's first name, usually abbreviated to an initial, and the names given at birth became the middle and last names. She figured Dr. A. Joseph Selvanathan must be his full name.

"Nirmala," she whispered, "is that your brother they're talking about, Dr. Selvanathan?"

"Yes, did not we tell you his complete name?"

"I can't remember. Maybe you did." Julia was beginning to dislike this Joseph even more. He would either be as aggressive and crude as Selvam, or else smug and self-righteous, perhaps both.

After dinner and after most of the guests had left, Julia joined the group in the main hall. She sat down next to Dr. Krishnamurthy from Udaipuram, a town about ten miles to the north. He was a middle-aged man with a hint of warmth behind his formal facade.

"Miss Julia," said the doctor, turning slightly toward her, "Dr. Arokiaswamy said you will leave soon."

"Yes, in about a month."

"What a loss. You have done so much for this area. Your idea to start a prenatal and neonatal care program, splendid idea. But then you have your own life back in the States to think of."

"I would like to stay, but so far I haven't found any way to do so."

"You would like to stay and work at the clinic?"

"Yes, but I can't get a government salary and the Peace Corps won't fund this area anymore. I was supposed to work my way out of a job by training others, but now it seems they are all going to take off in different directions. Even Rita will be getting married soon."

Dr. Arokiaswamy looked at Julia from across the room. His ashen face showed astonishment at what she had said. "You mentioned about Rita . . ."

"Yes. She said she'd be getting married soon." Julia hated to put Dr. Arokiaswamy on the spot. She had intended to confront Joseph, the source of the problem. But it happened to come up naturally in the conversation, and she felt Dr. Arokiaswamy should know about Rita's wrong idea.

"But I'm sure you are mistaken. Young girls do talk too much," said Dr. Arokiaswamy.

Julia could have added that Rita had even spoken of arrangements being made, but it would have been terribly embarrassing for the doctor, and rude on her part, so she added instead, "Maybe it was Lata who spoke of marriage."

As the others were leaving, Dr. Arokiaswamy asked Julia to stay a few minutes. When they were alone he asked, "What did Rita tell you?"

"That arrangements were being made for her wedding. It seems your son has indicated that he's planning to marry her," said Julia as gently as possible.

Dr. Arokiaswamy shook his head slowly. His whole face became drawn, focusing on the painful problem.

"Is there anything I can do to help?" offered Julia.

"No, there is nothing, Miss Julia. These are all family matters. Only, when my son returns from his friend's wedding, I wish that you do not discuss this with him. We must keep him in good humor."

Julia agreed because she couldn't refuse Dr. Arokiaswamy anything, and she didn't want to complicate family problems. She had never seen the doctor so upset, so helpless. It seemed as if he were carrying by far the greatest weight of sorrow. Julia saw in his face that the problems ran deeper than she had suspected. She utterly despised this Joseph Selvanathan. He was hurting all the people she loved and respected. And now, having given her word to Dr. Arokiaswamy, she wouldn't even get the satisfaction of telling this Joseph off to his face.

FOUR

Next morning's sick call at the clinic was very hectic, typical for a Monday. About twenty-five people came and sat on the veranda waiting benches. Leela combed out the most severe cases and gave them priority. The severity of some of the diseases was due to lack of immediate medical care.

One problem was that patients frequently used home cures first, which sometimes worked, and sometimes did not. And then many went to the local folk practitioners for a cure, each with his varying degree of success. Some were more like witch doctors—a few chants and shaking of margosa leaves for scorpion bites—while others had a deep knowledge of either the ancient Ayurvedic or Tamil medical systems. In too many cases, however, the home cures and visits to local practitioners just served to prolong the time before the patient, with an advanced or acute condition, finally approached the clinic.

One old woman squatting under a banyan tree in the clinic courtyard came to the clinic once or twice a week from a village six miles away. She had let some quacks perform cataract operations on both her eyes in the middle of a dusty village road. As a result she had become almost totally blind, and nothing could be done about it. She came just to get the experienced touch of Dr. Arokiaswamy with the hope that her sight would be restored. After Julia had come to the clinic, the old woman also asked for the American sister, thinking she may have better medicine.

In the morning the doctor had to perform two minor surgeries. Julia, Rita, and Dr. Rajan from a nearby town assisted, while Leela and the other nurses and students took care of both the inpatients and outpatients. By noon the staff had thirty minutes to eat their lunch, prepared by the clinic commissary, and it was one o'clock when Dr. Arokiaswamy and Julia went for village sick calls. Three afternoons a week they would travel to different villages.

Until recently Julia had been conducting health care workshops for the villagers, and training student nurses to conduct such classes, in accordance with her main duties as a Peace Corps worker. She had worked only part time as a regular nurse. Since she was scheduled to leave soon, she had wound up the workshops and had filled in full time as a nurse at the clinic and villages.

Today they visited a small village about eight miles west of the clinic. Dr. Arokiaswamy and Julia worked on the village headman's veranda, which had been closed on one end with palm thatch, just for the doctor. The villagers clustered around below, while one by one the sick ones came to the doctor.

Because only seven patients came with mild conditions, they were able to leave quite early. But before leaving the village, they stopped by the *cheri*, the untouchable hamlet, where the doctor treated four more patients. The untouchables were not allowed to go onto the headman's veranda.

On the way back to the clinic Dr. Arokiaswamy remained silent at first, and Julia felt that something troubled him. Finally he cleared his throat and spoke softly in his Tamil-mixed-with-British accent.

62

"My son has come back, as you know. It will mean a great deal for the clinic. Not every time can we have a doctor with his qualifications."

"Yes, indeed we're lucky." Julia quashed the sarcasm in her voice. Professionally speaking they were lucky, and she would do nothing to upset the doctor by showing contempt for his son.

"I am due to retire this year and go into a small private practice in Madras," continued the doctor. "The government has already given me two extensions. They would not allow the clinic to go without a doctor, but it is very hard for them to attract first-class doctors to the rural parts. You know all this."

"Yes," said Julia with a heavy voice. In many cases doctors who could not obtain work in more favorable locations or in private practice ended up in rural areas. Once there they constantly tried to find work in the cities and towns.

"My biggest worry has been about the qualifications of the doctor who replaces me, and about his attitude and dedication."

"Yes, I understand very well," said Julia. "Most doctors wouldn't make village sick calls, not to the extent that you do." She admired him so much. He was like a medical missionary in his own country.

"I built up the clinic, and my father before me, with much of our own money. I do not mean that I am a big man."

"But you are a big man," said Julia.

He smiled slightly. "I just do not want to see the clinic go down."

"But your son has come." Julia doubted he would be as dedicated as his father.

"Yes, and it has been the greatest joy in my life. I never

expected him to come back, even for a visit. He came for Nirmala's wedding, but he told me privately that he has no intention of staying."

"Oh?" said Julia, "Nirmala said—"

"Nirmala sometimes jumps ahead. She doesn't know about the family problems, since she was born much later."

So, there definitely were some family problems, thought Julia. "Then he won't stay?" she asked.

"He wants to return to America. He said he has become very accustomed to life there. He does not realize about our rural medical situation here. I implored him to stay and take over my practice. He said he would have to think about it, but meanwhile he will help me at the clinic during his six weeks' leave."

"Then, if he doesn't stay, it could be a great blow to the clinic, with you retiring and all."

"That is why it is so important. . . ." Dr. Arokiaswamy hesitated. "So important that all of us put forth efforts to make him happy and make him want to stay. We must all be kind to him, and encouraging. You especially could be very helpful in this matter, Miss Julia."

"In what way, Doctor?"

"It would be a good example for him to see how you, who were raised as an American, have adjusted so well to this country."

Julia realized Dr. Arokiaswamy was right, as much as she had already started disliking his son. It would be difficult to act nice to Joseph, since her true feelings usually became obvious. This last month in India might prove to be a most trying time. "I'll do my best," she assured Dr. Arokiaswamy.

"And please do not mention about Rita, as I said last night."

"No, I promise."

"Joseph is very sensitive about marriage. He always has been, so it is better we should avoid the subject completely." Dr. Arokiaswamy paused. His voice trembled slightly when he added, "He is a very good man. He is not to be blamed for anything."

Oh, sure, thought Julia. She felt quite disgusted hearing about how good this Joseph was when everything about him, all the harm he had done and was doing to Rita and Dr. Arokiaswamy, added up to an arrogant, selfish, and difficult person. If he were in love with some other woman, she would certainly understand why he didn't want to marry Rita. But he wasn't. He wanted an arranged marriage with some lady doctor—any lady doctor as long as she was of his same caste and rich! Again Julia thought how difficult being kind and polite to such a man might prove to be, and with that final thought they arrived back at the clinic.

Since it was only three thirty and Julia had no further work, she decided to go to the beach. There may not be many more chances to go there, she thought, as she fingered her bikini in her almirah. She had brought the bathing suit to India with the idea that swimming would help her survive the hot climate. That was before she had found out how modest the women were, before she herself had become so modest.

Of course, it would be quite a scandal if anyone in the area were to see her wearing a bikini, but she knew a beach where no one ever went only five miles east of the clinic. Even the people from the tourist lodge to the south never ventured there.

Julia changed into her bathing suit and put a red-and-brown batik cotton sari on top of it. Ordinarily she would have worn slacks, but today she was in the mood to wear a sari. That mood came over her more and more as the time drew near for her to leave India. She'd hardly get a chance to wear saris back in America.

She grabbed a towel and suntan lotion. After informing Leela where she was going, she climbed onto her bicycle and rode off down the dirt road. Her long, dark ponytail swayed gently on her back.

It was a glorious day, with at least two more hours of sunlight left. The scorching midday heat had evaporated in the warm breeze. Julia pushed all unpleasant thoughts out of her mind and savored the small, beautiful experiences of the moment. She even sang to herself as she cycled through the leafy arcade of tamarind trees.

The road was alive with people—people walking, driving bullock carts, riding cycles. The men wore ankle length wrap-around *kailis* of multicolored print or white cotton *dhotis*. The women wore cotton saris, some with the sari ends coiled on their heads to soften the pressure from the heavy bundles or pots they balanced gracefully. She waved to them and they waved back. They all knew the nurse from America, and Julia knew many of them.

Within twenty minutes of riding down several roads, the last one desolate and badly eroded from years of neglect, Julia had cycled as close as she could. She left the narrow road and walked her bicycle the last hundred yards through a sandy field of palm, coconut, and casuarina trees, avoiding the thick overgrowth of thorny bushes.

Finally the brush ended and a wide beach of coarse, white sand spread out to the east, about one hundred and fifty yards of it to the shoreline. The waves pounded and roared as they rushed quickly forward, then retreated with equally great force.

Julia walked onto the beach, down past the sharp incline where she could have privacy in case some villagers came to the field to gather firewood from the casuarina trees. She unwound her sari and took off her blouse. To counteract-feeling indecent in her bikini, she imagined herself in a different world, where she was the solitary inhabitant—stranded on a paradise island. Everyone needs a world like that, she thought, a place of their own—good therapy.

After spreading the towel she sat down. Pulling her long ponytail, which had settled between her well-curved breasts, behind her head, she lay back on the towel. She felt content to sunbathe, afraid to swim because of the violent waves.

The late afternoon sun clothed her in warmth, and she let herself drift into a light sleep. The rhythmical roaring of the waves gave the sensation of being rocked in a cradle.

She didn't know how much time had passed when she sensed through her closed eyelids the sky becoming suddenly darker. A cloud, she thought. But such dark clouds didn't usually come in the dry season. Before she could open her eyes she heard the voice.

"My lovely apparition."

Her eyes sprung wide. Between her and the westerly sun stood what seemed a giant just a few inches from her head. She couldn't make out the face at first because the sun was directly behind it, but she knew who it was by his soft, deep voice.

"You!" she exclaimed angrily, as she sat up and whirled around to face him.

Selvam stood motionless in his black swimming trunks which matched the black hair on his head and on his broad chest. His eyes danced merrily over her lightly clad body, stopping at her feminine curves. He licked his lip with a quick lash of the tongue and smiled.

Julia instinctively reached for her sari. How had he

found her? Ideas raced through her mind. He had found out her address from the hotel in Madras. Then he had come to the clinic. Leela was the only one who knew where she was. He had asked her. It would be all over the clinic about how a man came looking for Julia. Leela wouldn't gossip about her, but if others had been present when Selvam had come, what then?

"An American girl so shy?" he teased as she pulled the sari to her body. "Now, what are you doing on my beach?" He was quite pleased with himself, with the situation, with his defeated victim—Julia wasn't quite sure which.

Stunned, she asked, "Your beach?"

"Well, not really mine, but I used to swim here years ago. My parents had forbidden me to swim. They were afraid I might drown, so I found this beach."

Julia looked at him with surprise. Perhaps he was from the large fishing town eleven miles down the beach, or from the tourist lodge even closer. If that were the case, then he probably didn't know where she lived.

"You didn't expect to find me here?" she asked through a tight throat.

"How could I expect to find you here? I came for a swim only, not to find pretty girls. How was I to know you have a liking for the ocean as I do? We didn't talk much in Madras. Remember, you ran off."

Julia thought it wise not to ask where he lived. She might have to supply similar information about herself. Her only thought now was escape. She swallowed hard and commanded, "Will you please go and leave me alone!"

"But I came for a swim. Why don't you join me?" His eyes traveled gleefully over her body.

"I'd like to get dressed," she said sternly. "So if you'd

just leave for a few minutes, or go elsewhere to swim, then *I* will leave."

"But you are dressed, is it not?" His lips drew into a devilish smile.

She could see she was getting nowhere with him, so she stood up, clutching the sari to her body. She turned her back on him, then proceeded to wrap the sari haphazardly around her.

"Julia," he said in a serious tone. "Why are you so angry? You act as though we're strangers." He paused and sighed. "I'll never understand women."

Julia finished wrapping the sari and was about to leave when he grabbed her around the waist and turned her toward him. The beach, her private paradise island, suddenly became sinister in its isolation. No one would hear her if she called for help. Her heart started palpitating wildly. One shouldn't struggle in these situations, she thought. It would only make matters worse.

"Julia, I've been thinking about you ever since we met." His voice was gentle, but his arms held her firmly.

She looked into his dark brown eyes—sensitive eyes contrasting with his brutishly handsome face—imploring him with her own frightened eyes. "Selvam, please let me go." Julia tried to remain calm and sensible, but the quaver in her voice betrayed her.

"Not until I get what I want," he said with determination. Then he pulled her more firmly toward him.

She was no match against his strength. "Selvam, please," she whimpered.

"Why do you tremble so? Hmm? I would never harm you, Julia." He moved one hand up and, placing it behind her head, held it with an iron grip. Then his lips descended to hers. His kiss was gentle, sensual.

Julia stood motionless, waiting for a chance to reason

with him, but soon she felt heat rising to her face and spreading through her body, heat in addition to the heat of the day. His kiss awakened new feelings in her, sending impulses throughout her body. Despite her anger, despite her hatred for him, her lips started to respond naturally, kissing him back, though she kept her arms rigidly to her sides. Slowly his kisses became harder, full of longing and passion. He molded her body against his.

Her awareness of the force which threatened to consume them both sent a sudden chill of fear to her heart, and the implication of what they were doing focused her mind away from her own budding desires. Against the hardness of his body, she felt the pain of wanting to stay in his embrace and feel the hunger in his lips, now traveling to her cheek and chin and throat, but she knew she must leave at once. She was no longer in her private world. In her mind the whole of Indian society surrounded and judged her. In their eyes this man was insulting her. She was obliged to discourage him or else bear the brand of loose woman.

Julia's hands went to his chest and lingered there just an instant, feeling the tangle of his hair and strong beat of his heart, before she pushed him with all her force. "Selvam, stop!" she commanded.

His lips left her throat and he released her slowly, more on his own power than from the power in her arms. "Good, Julia! You should know I don't like women who easily acquiesce."

How many girls had easily acquiesced to him, she wondered, then stared at him harshly. "You think you are some god, a Krishna with Gopi cowherd girls ready to throw themselves at your feet!"

He laughed. She picked up her towel and blouse, and angrily pulled the sari end more firmly across her chest,

70

over her shoulder and around in front, tucking it in. Walking as fast as she could through the sinking sand, she half-expected Selvam to follow after her.

But Selvam stood his ground, and when she turned to look at him, he was smiling. His arms were crossed in front of him and his black hair fell across his forehead in a way that made her breath catch, as it had before in Madras, and always would . . . if she were ever to see him again.

She turned away from him and continued toward her bicycle. His voice rang deep and clear: "I like a challenge. Your recalcitrant behavior only makes me more ardent."

Recalcitrant behavior! As if she were some rebellious criminal, as if she were in the wrong. Fury whipped through her. She angrily grabbed her bicycle and walked it through the field, then rode it as quickly as she could down the dirt road, pushing with all her weight on the pedals. She felt so angry, she didn't think about how strange it was that he had made an indirect threat to pursue her, and yet did not pursue her.

In a few minutes Julia had traveled some distance over the eroded, rock-infested road. In her distressed state she had not taken care to wrap her sari properly. Suddenly the bicycle jerked to a halt. Julia felt herself being flung into the air. The world circled upside down until she crashed to the ground. Her whole body at first seemed numb, then instantly her knee shot with pain.

The front wheel of her cycle spun freely, suspended in the air. She wondered what had happened. Then as her dazed state eased, she saw the end of her sari stuck in the spokes of the rear wheel. "Ooh!" She grasped her knee. Blood was coming through her sari.

On the road just beside her the sharp edge of a half-buried stone jutted up from the reddish earth. She pulled herself over to the cycle. It took a few minutes to free her sari from the spokes. Then with great difficulty she stood up and brought the cycle to an upright position.

In the distance Selvam came walking. He now wore slacks and a shirt.

"Julia!" he shouted when he saw her. Then he began to run toward her.

Fear startled Julia's senses. Her only thought—Selvam must not know where she lived. With strength gained from panic she climbed back on her cycle and rode away from a man who wouldn't harm her—she knew that instinctively—away from a man who might even help her.

In twenty minutes, as soon as the clinic compound came into view, the pain in Julia's knee overcame her. The last few yards were sheer torture as she cycled up to her small house.

From the distance Rita, Susheela, and Lata, her three student nurses, waved at her. They apparently didn't see the blood on her sari. She waved back and worked on unlocking the rusty padlock. On the other side of the duplex she could hear Raman and Leela through the iron-grilled window speaking in Tamil about going to see Dr. Arokiaswamy's son, who had just returned from his friend's wedding.

Julia left her cycle on the narrow screened-in porch, entered her home, and flicked on the light in her small living room. The room was stark, with only two chairs. No pictures on her powder blue walls, only a mirror—quite the opposite to Leela and Raman's home on the other side. Their walls were cluttered, just like Dr. Arokiaswamy's, with family and religious pictures. The only difference was their pictures were of Hindu gods and goddesses rather than Christian saints.

Julia limped to the bathroom. She knew the cut was

serious enough to call the doctor, but decided to wait until tomorrow. Her emotions seemed so jumbled, she didn't feel like facing anyone. Leela would see through her and suspect that something more than a wound troubled her. Dr. Arokiaswamy would be with his son, and she didn't want to disturb them.

Julia dressed the wound with a handkerchief, changed into a robe, and sank down onto her narrow, wooden cot. Though it was quite early in the evening, an overwhelming weariness consumed her and she fell asleep.

FIVE

"Leela," called Julia. It was six thirty in the morning. Julia waited. She knew Leela was up. She had heard water running. "Leela," she called again after a few minutes.

Leela came rushing over. Julia limped to the door with pain shooting through her leg. "Please send for Dr. Arokiaswamy. I really should have seen him last night." Julia lifted her robe to reveal the swollen, festered wound with a blood-soaked handkerchief for a dressing.

"Oh, Julia, why you did not tell us?" Leela wrinkled her brow.

"I didn't think it was that bad and I didn't want to disturb anyone, especially with Dr. Arokiaswamy's son just returned."

"I will go bring the doctor this moment." She was gone before Julia could sit down again.

Half an hour later Dr. Arokiaswamy entered. Julia, sitting in a rosewood armchair, raised her robe and showed him the wound. The doctor knelt down, bending his head over it, so that all Julia could see was his white crop of hair. "Why you did not call me last night?" he asked. "Just now I have another emergency. Mrs. Jayaraman is in labor. But my son is coming to attend you. He is a fine doctor." Dr. Arokiaswamy was very apologetic that he wouldn't be able to treat Julia personally.

"Yes, I'm sure he's very good." Julia didn't want to meet him this way, not as his patient.

Just then footsteps outside her door caught her attention. In stepped the overbearing figure of Selvam with a white medical coat over his clothes and a black doctor's bag in his hand. The gold block initials on the bag read, A.J.S. Julia stared in disbelief. Her pretty mouth opened a bit and her throat muscles tightened. Strangely Selvam didn't seem to show any surprise in seeing her.

"Miss Julia," said Dr. Arokiaswamy, standing up, "this is my son, Dr. A. Joseph Selvanathan. Joseph, please meet our most valuable nurse, Miss Julia Cairns. She has done an excellent job training the student nurses, including our Rita."

Selvam pressed the palms of his hands together and bowed slightly in the traditional Indian greeting. Julia did the same, thinking it humorously bizarre to be so formal with a man who had kissed her just the previous day. But she didn't smile at the man she had come to detest. The heat of embarrassment turned her cheeks red with the thought of what Dr. Arokiaswamy would think if he knew about the events leading to her careless ride home.

Selvam spoke in a detached manner. "Yes, I've heard much about her from your letters and Nirmala's. Even Leela and Rita wrote about her."

Dr. Arokiaswamy looked at the slight smile on his son's face and then looked at Julia who was still blushing. The moment hung heavily, waiting for some action. Then, to Julia's relief, Dr. Arokiaswamy made apologies and left for the clinic.

Leela and Raman, who had entered the room just after Selvam, circled around while Selvam knelt to the ground. Julia slowly drew her robe up just above the wound on her knee. Selvam became immediately irritated and pushed it up farther with a certain roughness. His head bent over her knee, and she marveled at his black hair gleaming in the morning sun which flooded in through her iron-grilled window. His kiss from the day before still burned on her lips despite her every effort to forget it.

Selvam looked up at Leela and Raman. "No need for you to stay. I can take care of this."

"Leela's a good nurse," suggested Julia. She didn't want to be left alone with Selvam—Dr. Selvanathan. She trusted his medical ability, she just didn't trust him.

Selvam almost laughed. "I very well know about Mrs. Ramanathan. She took care of me many times when I was a child."

Leela beamed. "Joseph was such a sweet baby."

Sure, thought Julia. *He was probably a little angel.* No one here would ever suspect what he's really like.

Raman and Leela said good-bye and left. Julia felt a confused flood of emotions. So this was Joseph, the man causing so much trouble for Dr. Arokiaswamy and Rita, and Joseph was Selvam, the man creating so much trouble for her. He had seen her under all the worst circumstances, first in the hotel lobby, where he had thought she was staring at him, then at the beach, where she was wearing her bikini, and now here, where she was a foolish nurse who couldn't even take care of herself. The anger, frustration, and shame were all too complicated for her to sort out at the moment. And his physical presence created other feelings she preferred not to think about.

He spoke with professional concern. "Let's go into your bathroom where I can wash the wound."

She nodded weakly and he took her hand, then pulled her up. Putting his arm around her, he pulled her against his side. It wasn't necessary, she thought. Because of the position he had her in, her body raised up against his, she had no other choice but to put her arm around his neck. This was the man she had vowed to hate, but with his warm body against hers, she felt tingly all over, and a little dizzy.

In the bathroom she sat on the edge of the small cement reservoir. He sat on the low bathroom stool and lifted up her robe. He poured water over the wound to soften the handkerchief which was stuck to the dried blood. Then he pulled it off slowly.

"Ouch!" she cried. A sting of tears came to her eyes and she braced her hands on his shoulders.

"A handkerchief!" he said harshly. "You might as well have spread a coating of staphylococcal bacteria on the wound. And that is just what you did! Better to have left it without a dressing." He looked up at her guilt-ridden face and added softly with a smile, "You foolish little girl."

She had been completely exhausted the previous evening. Her mind had been in a daze. But that was no excuse for a nurse, she reprimanded herself, not for a nurse who had just spent two years trying to teach villagers about the germ theory. Then she remembered that this whole problem with the wound was largely his fault. Then why did he seem so much in the right, and she so much in the wrong?

He scrubbed the wound with antibacterial soap. It hurt. Her hands tightened on his shoulders. He was very rough, necessarily so to clean out the wound, but he seemed to enjoy hurting her. Revenge for her unwillingness to cooperate with him, she thought. She bitterly endured the pain, thinking that perhaps she was giving him just a little pain by gripping his shoulders so tightly.

After the scrubbing he flooded the wound with rubbing

alcohol, then applied a thick layer of antibiotic cream and dressed the wound with a gauze and tape bandage.

"I think you'll survive," was his facetious prognosis. He helped her to the bedroom cot. His large body made the small room seem so much smaller, and his thick deep voice reverberated off the walls. "You should take the day off today. Tomorrow, we'll see about it."

"But there's so much work. I can't just take off for a silly cut."

"Do you mean to disobey your doctor? Do you doubt my judgment?" he asked with mock indignation.

"No . . . no . . . but the clinic . . ."

"You forget that I'm here now. I'll take care of the clinic."

"Yes, of course." She thought of how he really didn't intend to stay and she wanted to call him an arrogant hypocrite, but then she remembered Dr. Arokiaswamy's request for her to be nice to him so that he would stay. She hated the way he always came out ahead.

"When was your last tetanus shot?" he asked in a professional tone.

"Oh, dear." A stretch of silence increased the tension. "I may have had one last month."

He looked at her impatiently. "Shall I go to the clinic and check your record?"

"No, I remember now. It was a cholera booster I had last month. I haven't had a tetanus shot for over a year."

"Are you quite certain?" He stood with his arms folded, the way he had when he had first stared at her from the hotel doorway.

"Yes, I'm positive. You don't have to doubt my word," she said acidly.

His voice softened, "I wouldn't want anything to happen to you, that's all." He reached into his black bag and pulled out a vial of antitoxin and a syringe. As he filled the syringe he spoke to her gently. "Julia, I know you're angry with me. I wish you'd trust me."

"That's your best line yet," she said caustically. Then she relented a little and asked, "How can I ever trust you?" She felt angry at the passion he had shown her and at the way he had been leading Rita on, while all along he planned to marry another woman, a lady doctor, as he had told his family.

"You'll learn," he said. "For now I wish you'd stop hating me. I'm not at all as bad as you think. I've never in my life done anything to a girl—unless she were willing." He dabbed some alcohol on her arm, then injected the needle. "And frankly, I've never known a girl who objected to being kissed."

Julia winced from the pain of the injection, and her blood boiled at what he had said. He was not only experienced with women, but also in playing games with them. He had said "unless she were willing." In other words, according to him, he could never be blamed for anything. The whole responsibility fell on his "willing" women. Well, she would certainly never show any willingness. Quite the contrary, she felt like ordering him out of her house and out of her life. But then Dr. Arokiaswamy had told her to be kind to him. Perhaps the future of the clinic was at stake. She couldn't simply tell him off as she so much wanted to do.

"I don't hate you . . ." she said in a deliberately indefinite tone. "But I'm not really your type of woman, and I wish to keep our relationship strictly professional, since it looks like we'll be working together."

"I'm glad you don't hate me, Miss Julia." By his voice she sensed he was already miles away from her and she somehow felt deserted. "Perhaps we could be friends."

Julia frowned.

"Strictly platonic, my dear Miss Julia." With all the bedside manner of an old-fashioned doctor he patted her leg and smiled. "Now, I suggest you stay off your feet as much as possible. I'll look in on you tomorrow, but if you notice any furthering of the infection, don't hesitate to call for me."

He packed his black bag. Julia felt it was safe to ask the question that had been bothering her ever since he had entered her house. "When you came here this morning you didn't seem surprised to see me. Did you know who I was . . . before?"

A very broad smile crossed his face. "When you told me your name in Madras I knew who you were. I knew all about you. That your mother was Indian. That you lived with your aunt and uncle in Milwaukee."

"Why didn't you tell me?" Her soft lips formed into a pout and she furrowed her brow.

"Because I wanted my arrival to be a surprise. And I wanted to find out more about you, after such praise from everyone here." He started to leave.

"Then what should I call you? Dr. Selvanathan or Joseph or Selvam?" asked Julia in a defeated voice. He was Selvam to her and always would be, but she felt confused now.

"Call me *athan.*"

"Don't tease me," said Julia, her heart pounding wildly. Since they were not cross cousins, *athan* would mean husband.

"If it would make you feel more comfortable, then call me Selvam. My mother called me Selvam."

She didn't remember Mrs. Arokiaswamy using any other name than Joseph, but she didn't question it. With all sincerity she said, "Thank you for treating my wound."

"Oh, no need to thank me," he said with a twinkle in his eye. "I'll be sending you the bill." He wheeled around and left her speechless and blushing.

At mid-morning someone knocked on Julia's door. "Yes?" she called.

"Sister. The doctor gave this for you."

"Come in, Siva," called Julia.

A boy about sixteen years old, looking more like thirteen, entered the room. He was barefooted and wore a faded shirt and khaki shorts. His legs and arms were very thin, but as with everything else in India, appearances were deceiving. He was actually quite strong. He held out a small package wrapped in white paper and string.

"The doctor?" Julia questioned.

"Yes, sister, the American doctor."

"Oh, you mean Dr. Selvanathan?"

"Yes, sister."

Julia opened the package and took out a paperback book, yellowed with age, entitled *Shilappadikaram (The Ankle Bracelet)* by Prince Ilango, adigal, translated into English. Julia contained any embarrassment because Siva still stood in front of her. She looked at him and said, "Thank you, Siva. You may go now."

Siva smiled. "Also he sent this, sister." He presented her with another package wrapped in a plantain leaf. Julia took it from Siva and blushed. It contained jasmine blossoms. She could tell by its light weight and the faint perfume which managed to find a way out of the packet. She set it on the table beside her.

"Thank you, Siva."

As Siva left, he asked, "You need something, sister? I can bring."

"No, thank you."

After Siva left, Julia started reading the book. The introduction explained that it was written around 171 A.D. by a Chera prince about a Chola husband and wife who met their fate in the Pandyan city of Madurai, thus including the three ancient and glorious kingdoms of the southernmost part of India, kingdoms that lived on in the pride of the people.

Another world, another layer to this land, thought Julia. Her awareness heightened to the realization that she was not only in India, not only in the State of Tamil Nadu and the district of South Arcot, but perhaps in some ways more significant in its subtleness she was in the heart of Chola country. She wondered what lesson Selvam was trying to teach her through this book. She thought he must be giving her some message. Curiosity, rather than a desire to please him, made her read further.

Julia had read about twenty pages when she heard the boisterous giggling of girls outside her door.

"Julia," said Rita, as she, Lata, and Susheela burst into her room, dressed in their white nurses' uniforms, "we brought your lunch."

Julia set the book down, delighted to see her three pupils. They set about opening up the steel tiffin carrier, one compartment with rice, one with *sambar,* a lentil and vegetable soup, another with cabbage seasoned with coconut and fried mustard seeds, and the last with some fried fish. Then Lata opened a plantain leaf packet of *mysore pak,* a very sugary sweet. They placed all the food on a stool in front of Julia.

Their oiled black hair was pulled neatly back into buns, as required for their nursing jobs, but Julia frowned at the jasmine chains around their hair. "I'm away one day, and you wear flowers in your hair. You know that nurses shouldn't wear flowers on the job."

"But, Julia," pleaded Lata, flashing her slightly bucked teeth, "we just put them on during the lunch hour. Dr. Selvanathan brought them for us. You know Dr. Selvanathan," she said looking toward Rita, "Rita's *athan.*"

Rita smiled and blushed while Lata and Susheela giggled mercilessly.

"Is he not just so handsome, Rita?" teased Lata.

"And he called her his *murai pon,*" chimed in Susheela, then she explained to Julia that it meant female in a marriagable relation. "And he asked Rita if she were ready for their wedding night, since he had been waiting some time for her to grow up," she said with glee.

"He is *so* handsome, and *so* naughty," said Lata emphatically.

"Do you know what Rita said?" asked Susheela making the most of the mirthful situation.

"No!" cried Rita unable to control her own smile. "Hush, Susheela."

"She said . . ." Susheela looked around, hesitating.

"She said," picked up Lata, "that she had been very well ready for some time, but she doubted that he was quite ready himself."

All three girls, including Rita, broke out with ribald laughter. Julia couldn't help but join in. She was, at this moment, happy that Selvam had met his match with earthy Rita. Then she remembered what Nirmala had told her, that Selvam had refused to marry Rita. Julia took a tone of seriousness. "Okay now, let me eat my lunch."

"What is this package?" asked Rita, picking up the jasmine packet and opening it. "Did Joe *athan,* I mean Dr. Selvanathan, bring you some flowers too?"

Susheela took the chain of flowers from Rita. "Let me put them in your hair."

Julia turned her head while Susheela drew some strands of hair just above Julia's braid. She doubled the flower chain twice and threaded it through the hair.

Julia ate some *mysore pak*. "This is excellent. Did Mrs. Arokiaswamy make it?"

"Oh, no," said Rita, "Joe *athan* brought it back from his friend's wedding. He told us to take some for you."

"He said," laughed Lata, "that you are too skinny and need to be fattened up." The girls burst out giggling again.

"Oh, he said that, did he?" replied Julia. All these years she had watched her diet to stay in good health and keep her trim but womanly figure, which was now being made the brunt of a joke by one arrogant, heartless man. She put the *mysore pak* down and wondered what exactly his motives were. Fatten her up like some little Gretel? What for?

A few hours after the girls had gone back to work, a car horn sounded outside Julia's house. It was about two in the afternoon and she expected no one. But the horn persisted. Julia limped to the door. Her leg felt much better since it had been treated that morning. As she crossed the threshhold, the bright sun hit her face. The bougainvillea vine over her head with its tissuelike blooms of an outrageous magenta hue offered no shade. She squinted. It was Selvam in his father's car, a cream-colored Ambassador.

"Leela said you know where Mr. Kumarswamy lives," he shouted.

"Which Kumarswamy?"

"The one in Udaipuram."

Julia gave a puzzled "yes."

"Come on, then. You'll have to show me," said Selvam

in a voice that would not accept a negative reply. "It seems his mother is ill. He phoned an hour ago, but I was in surgery." He spoke rapidly. "My father and Arul are over at some village. Ramanathan is away."

Julia heard the urgency in his voice. She felt totally unprepared in her cotton house sari which she had just changed into. Her hair needed to be combed and rebraided —loose sable strands cupped her face—and she didn't have a bit of makeup on. Her aunt used to scold, "Julia, you look undressed. Put on a little lipstick before you leave the house." But Julia didn't give her appearance a second thought as she slipped on her sandals near the door. She limped over to the car and climbed in next to Selvam.

They were off down the road, speeding over bumps and chuckholes, blowing up dust in their wake.

"It sure is hard to get used to driving on the left side," commented Selvam.

"But surely it would come back to you easily. After all you've only been gone six years, haven't you?"

"Huh? Six years? No, I just came back for a short visit then."

"Oh, I thought you said . . ."

"Now which way do I turn?"

"Left." They turned onto a blacktop road, almost as bumpy as the dirt road, but much more pleasant because tamarind trees shaded it on either side.

Selvam had difficulty dodging in and out among bullock carts stacked high with straw, bicycles, barefooted pedestrians, stray animals, cars which came head on in the middle of the road in a battle of nerves to see which car would have to pass partly on the shoulder, and those "bloody" lorries, as Arul referred to them. Lorry drivers not only thought they owned the road as did every other wayfarer, but their lorries were just big and sturdy enough to give them the confidence that they would come out relatively unharmed in any collision.

The car nearly hit a goat that had suddenly dashed out in front of them. Selvam slammed on the brakes and the whole herd and its herder, clad in a loincloth and wielding a long walking stick, claimed the road. Julia, who had braced herself in automatic reflex, looked at Selvam with amazement. "You're going to have to use the horn," she said.

"It seems indecent," replied Selvam. She continued to look at him. He obviously had never driven in India before.

Selvam pressed the horn and inched his way through the herd.

"I thought you drove to your friend's wedding," she said.

"Arul drove."

Once past the herd of goats they picked up speed. He blasted the horn at some pedestrians carrying huge bundles of sticks on their heads. They slowly moved over just in time for him to pass them without going off the road.

"Turn right up there, on that road just past the mud hut," said Julia.

Selvam turned. Coconut trees lined this road. Beyond the trees were dry rice paddy fields which would spring forth with verdant rice shoots once the planting season had begun, after the dry wedding season ended. Julia felt a little sad at the thought that she wouldn't be here to see the velvet green of another paddy crop.

"Then how long have you been in America?" Julia asked.

"I left India fifteen years ago when I was seventeen. I

went as an exchange student my last year in high school, so one might say I practically grew up in America."

Julia began to understand. Selvam was more Americanized than she had suspected. Perhaps, just perhaps, he had not really been insulting her by his male aggression, at least not any more than an American man. Without thinking of the importance of the question, she asked, "Are you planning to stay here at the clinic?"

"Do you want me to stay?" he asked in a completely serious voice. He turned for a brief moment and looked at her, piercing her with the question. His face was so compelling, so brooding, and so handsome. Everything seemed to hinge on Julia's response. Would he stay if she said she wanted him to? She sensed that he might. But what did he expect of her in return? Platonic friendship? She doubted that.

Suddenly the town appeared before them. The top of the steep sloping Hindu temple, ornamented with multicolored figures of gods, goddesses, sacred animals, kings, and warriors, hovered above the red-tiled roofs.

SIX

Udaipuram was a small town, just four or five concentric squares of streets with houses and shops surrounding the temple. Julia directed Selvam to Mr. Kumarswamy's house where a male servant waited for them on the small, pillared veranda. They entered through the narrow hall and Julia slipped off her sandals, according to custom. The hall opened into an expansive cement-floored living room with a large opening in the roof to let in light and air, and a slightly sunken area below the opening to drain off rain water. Doors on all sides of the room led to smaller, darker rooms.

Kumarswamy, almost as tall as Selvam but thinner and a few years younger, paced back and forth. He stopped when they entered.

"Dr. Selvanathan?"

"Yes, Mr. Kumarswamy?" The two men silently stared at each other, a little longer, thought Julia, than two strangers normally would stare.

"My mother," said Kumarswamy, "has been giddy all day."

"Your mother . . . Kavitha, I believe?" said Selvam.

"You know her?" Kumarswamy seemed to gasp.

"But who has not heard of the famous Kavitha? I saw her on stage when I was very young. An exquisite Bharatanatyam dancer." Selvam spoke with a slightly rigid jaw.

"She has been having high blood pressure these past five years." Kumarswamy sounded worried.

"Well, then, let me have a look at her."

"Please excuse me, Miss Julia, for being so taken up," said Kumarswamy, turning to Julia, who had been standing at a distance. "How are you?" His dark, liquid gaze lingered on her.

"Fine," she said weakly. Selvam's dark brown eyes, which seemed black at the moment, darted toward Julia, burning into her. She remembered how jealous he had been about the rickshaw man in Madras. "I came here several times with Dr. Arokiaswamy," offered Julia to Selvam with a tremble in her voice. Then she reprimanded herself for allowing him to make her feel guilty.

Selvam, doctor's bag in hand, and Julia followed Kumarswamy across the wide room to a heavy woman in her late fifties, leaning back in a rattan easy chair. She was breathing irregularly and her head hung slightly to one side.

"*Amma,*" said Kumarswamy in Tamil, "this is Dr. Selvanathan. He will help you."

She answered in Tamil, not looking at Selvam, "Where is Dr. Arokiaswamy?"

"*Amma,*" said Kumarswamy, "Dr. Selvanathan is Dr. Arokiaswamy's son. The doctor is away from the clinic. I'm sure Dr. Selvanathan is just as good as his father."

The aging Kavitha looked up at Selvam. "My blood pressure," she said in English with a very thick accent.

Selvam took out his sphygmomanometer and stethoscope from the bag and took her blood pressure. Then he checked her other vital signs, and continued to examine her for about fifteen minutes. He turned to Kumarswamy when he was finished.

"Her blood pressure is fine right now. Of course it could have been up earlier. I can't find anything else wrong with her. It may be the heat. You really should see Dr. Krishnamurthy here in town."

"My mother trusts only Dr. Arokiaswamy."

"We are quite busy out at the clinic," said Selvam. He packed his bag and was getting ready to leave. A young servant girl in a printed, ankle-length skirt and nylon half sari—only three yards long instead of the six yards in a full sari—beamed a toothy smile, as she entered with a tray of lemonade.

"Please sit down, Dr. Selvanathan," said Kumarswamy.

"I really must rush," said Selvam. "I left the clinic without a doctor. May I use your phone?"

"Certainly." Kumarswamy led him to the telephone. Selvam called the clinic and spoke in Tamil to his father, who had returned by then.

Julia and Selvam drank the lemonade. It had ice in it, a sign that the family had a refrigerator and was somewhat wealthy. Then they left without the usual formalities of lingering and continuing the conversation. Quite obviously Selvam wanted to break away as quickly as he could.

Back on the road, however, his mood changed. He winked at Julia and asked, "How would you like that wound to heal very quickly?"

"How is that possible?"

"We'll go to the ocean. There's nothing better than salt water."

Julia's heart beat loudly. She didn't know what Selvam had in mind, but she guided him to their private beach anyway, not quite sure whether she was doing the right thing.

He parked as close as they could get by car. "I'll go change into my trunks," he said.

"Your trunks? You planned to come here?" she said with a swallow.

"The thought had crossed my mind."

She couldn't understand why she was letting Selvam lead her on. The memory of his kiss the previous day still tormented her. She didn't want anything like that to happen again. It would create an extremely awkward situation at the clinic. On the other hand he had indicated he wouldn't force himself on her. He had said their relationship would be platonic.

"I didn't bring my bathing suit," she offered as an excuse to get out of a situation she felt had become dangerous. She couldn't run away this time, not with her leg still sore.

"Improvise," he said flippantly.

"What do you mean?"

He saw the worry spreading across her face. "Julia, trust me. I won't harm you. I'm only thinking of your wound. The salt water is very good for healing wounds. Now, do you know how village girls bathe in irrigation canals and tanks?"

"Yes." She had seen them sometimes. They would wear their sari petticoats tied up above their breasts.

"Do you think you could do that?"

Julia remained silent, contemplating whether or not to demand that they return immediately to the clinic.

"Come on, Julia, you'd be more covered up than in that bikini of yours."

"All right," she said slowly, "but where should I dress?"

"There are plently of trees and shrubs around here. I'll guard you."

Julia had no fear of other people coming. She had never seen others there. She was afraid of Selvam, but he did seem sincere. She got out of the car and went into a cluster of shrubs nearby. In a few minutes she emerged dressed in what looked like a white cotton tent extending from above her shapely breasts where she had tightly tied the drawstring down to just below her knees. Selvam came toward her in his black swimming trunks which contrasted with his golden tan body. A gold chain around his neck gleamed in the sun.

They put their clothes in the dicky, and Selvam got a safety pin from Julia and pinned the key to the dicky on his chain. Then, before Julia could protest, he lifted her up in his arms with the ease of an eagle swooping down to catch a sparrow in its talons. As an automatic reflex she clung to his neck.

"This isn't necessary," she said. "I can walk."

"Oh, but it is necessary. And you can't walk very well, can you?" he replied, smiling at her.

Only now Julia realized how very strong Selvam was as he carried her through the fields of bushes and casuarina trees, much stronger than she had imagined.

"When I fatten you up," he said in a happy mood, "I won't be able to carry you so easily."

"I don't want to get fat," protested Julia.

"But you'd be so much more beautiful. Of course you do have a nice figure, but Indian men like women a little plump."

"I'm an American and I like to be thin," she said indignantly.

"But you're half Indian, is it not? We shall see then after

93

a few years whether you put on a little extra weight. It's biologically adaptive to have a few extra pounds here."

A few years, she thought. She wouldn't be here. She felt sort of glad now that she'd be leaving in a month. Selvam's arrival at the clinic had created an embarrassing situation for her. Even if he were safely married to an educated, rich woman in his caste, as he had specified to his parents, the experiences they had shared in the last few days couldn't be erased. Nor could Julia quiet the feelings that sprung forth in her heart, despite all rational arguments against them. She knew it would be best for her to leave India, but for now she rested her head against his shoulder and closed her eyes. He looked down on her face with a satisfied smile.

Close to the shore line, where the sand was damp and firm, he let her down. Then he kneeled on one knee and took off her dressing. She resisted the impulse to rake her fingers through his blue-black hair. He threw the dressing to the ground and stood up, offering his hand. She hesitated. "Come on, I won't bite you," he said, smiling.

"I just came here before to sunbathe. I've never gone swimming in the ocean."

"That's right, you're from Wisconsin. Well, I went to college in California, so I've been swimming in the ocean all my life. It's one of my greatest pleasures. Come, we'll just wade today."

His large hand enveloped her small one and he led her into the surf. The water felt warm compared to the rivers and lakes she had swum in, but it felt refreshingly cool in contrast to the oven-heat of the air.

The waves were so powerful Julia nearly fell down. Selvam kept a tight grip on her, hurting her hand. The sand in the water hit her with blasting force. At first it stung her wound, the salt and sand, but in a few minutes the pain decreased.

Before long they were wet up to their waists with the broken waves hitting them. The pull of the retreating surf equaled the force of the oncoming waves. Julia felt she might be sucked into the deep waters of the ocean, but Selvam held her tightly. Again she became acutely aware of his strength and solid, lean weight. Even so, he also had to struggle a bit to keep his balance.

A very large wave broke. Julia could see it coming. When it hit, it tore her away from Selvam. She almost fell when his arm encircled her waist. He pulled her toward him so that he held her back against his body, his arm clamped just below her breasts. He would certainly be able to feel her heart beating rapidly, she thought. She struggled a little. He held her more tightly.

"Shouldn't we go back now?" she asked, pressing her head against his shoulder. She could feel his heavy breath.

"No," he murmured close to her ear. "It's better to stay longer." His lips were close to her face. She couldn't tell whether he was gently kissing her or whether the motion of the surf made his lips brush against her temple.

Then he asked, "Do you enjoy it?"

Her cheeks reddened. Did he mean the water or being held in his arms? She replied, "Yes. I enjoy the ocean very much."

"Good," he said softly, "then we can come here often. It's not fun to swim alone. It's even dangerous in these waters." He released her, dipped his hand in the water, and stroked her hot face, wetting it. Then he pushed a few stray hairs back from her cheeks. "How does that feel?"

It felt good, refreshing. Julia suddenly had the idea. The water waited for someone to splash it, almost begged to be splashed. She cupped her hands and dished up some foamy water right into Selvam's face. "How does that feel?" she asked with a pretty, witchlike smile.

He stood wet-faced. The muscles in his angular jaws rippled. "It looks like you need to be baptized in the ocean."

"No," she squealed, trying to run from him.

He caught her immediately and swung her up in his arms.

"Put me down," she demanded in mock seriousness, hitting her clenched fists on his shoulder.

"I will." He dropped her in the water. She went all the way under, then came up wet head to toe. She stayed in the water, letting it cover her up to her neck. It felt wonderful. "It's not fair," she said waving her arms to keep her balance. "You're stronger than I am."

"Then I'll join you." He dove in and came up behind her, grabbing her toe. She cried out in delight. She couldn't remember ever having so much fun—all past problems forgotten for the moment. They splashed and laughed.

"It's good to see you happy, *ma,*" said Selvam.

It felt good to be happy, thought Julia. It had been a long time since she had been so happy. Or had she ever been so happy?

"And you're always happy," she said. "Always with a zeal for life." Despite whatever else she felt for him, anger, contempt . . . attraction, she had from the time she met him been aware of, had even been overwhelmed by, his magnetic energy.

"My life hasn't been happy," said Selvam. With those few words the moment was irretrievably lost, the magic broken.

What he had said pierced her through and through. Why had his life been unhappy? Her first reaction—poor

96

little rich boy—was immediately replaced with compassion, the same compassion that had led her to take up the nursing profession. He was like a wounded little boy, crying to be hugged and caressed. She felt so confused in her loathing for him, and attraction, and now compassion.

They stayed in the water a little longer and then Julia suggested, "Perhaps we should go now." She held up her fingers, deeply wrinkled by the water, and forced a smile.

"Now we are old people," said Selvam, in a dramatically humorous voice. "We spent our entire lifetimes in the ocean."

"Was it a waste of time?" asked Julia. Her question, meant in pure jest, was out before the echo of it came back to her in a hauntingly serious tone.

"No, dear, it wasn't a waste. We were together, is it not?" Selvam took her two hands and kissed one, then the other.

As he looked down at her, she saw unmistakable tenderness in his dark eyes, sparkling like a breeze-blown pond. Could she be falling in love with this complete scoundrel? she wondered. Impossible. And yet she was beginning to feel something more than mere attraction. Perhaps a sense of attachment? It couldn't be love, she reasoned, not for a man as despicable as Selvam.

By the time they reached the car, the scorching heat of the day had almost dried them. Despite that, Julia shivered. Sensing her apprehension about him, Selvam stroked her head and soothed, "Everything will be all right for us."

Julia remained silent, not knowing what to say, but thinking about what he could mean by "for us."

After they dressed and Selvam put cream and a fresh bandage on her wound, they were off again, bumping over potholes and stones, down the dirt road.

He pulled a cigarette pack out of his chest pocket and offered it to Julia.

"No, thanks, I don't smoke."

"Good, Julia. You're quite sensible. I'm not so sensible. Hope you don't mind." Selvam lit a cigarette for himself and took a long drag on it.

"Where are we going?" asked Julia when he failed to turn.

"I thought we would stop by the beach resort and get something to eat. I know my way from here."

"I'm not hungry." It was drawing near tiffin time, but Julia just wanted to return home.

"Well, perhaps you won't mind if I eat. I didn't have lunch today because I was in surgery, C-section for Mrs. Jayaraman."

Julia suddenly felt selfish. She had only been thinking of herself, her feelings. Selvam also had feelings and needs. "No, of course not," she said meekly. "I don't mind."

"Did you read *Shilappadikaram?*" he asked, turning to look at her briefly with a dark flash of his eyes.

"I've read about thirty pages so far."

"And what do you think of it?"

"It's beautifully written, the poetry and prose."

"And what about the story?"

So he did want her to learn something. "Well, I've only gotten to the part where Kovalan forsakes his wife, Kannaki, for the beautiful courtesan dancer, Madhavi. I didn't realize the ancient literature of India could be so . . ." She thought of saying "sensual," but instead added "romantic."

"Actually, you have to read the whole book to realize how relevant it is for life in India."

"Of course things were quite different then, I mean from the present," said Julia.

98

"In what way?"

"Well, they seem to have been a little morally lax. For example, there were courtesan dancers then, mistresses of the wealthy men and nobles."

"And what makes you think there are no courtesans today?"

"I . . . I just assumed. I mean Indians seem to be so . . . so . . ."

"Moral?" laughed Selvam. "There are a lot of things you don't know about India. Up until recently we had a courtesan dancer caste. Now as a caste, at least, they have given up their, shall we say, past habits? But I can assure you we still have our courtesans, probably from every caste, and perhaps in as plentiful supply as in ancient times. And we also have our keeps."

"It's very difficult for me to believe that." Julia felt bewildered by this new piece of knowledge.

"Of course, it's not advertised, but they do exist. Kavitha, for example, is the keep of a wealthy man. Didn't you notice all her jewelry? The tip of an iceberg, I imagine. She's been very well kept, is it not?"

"Now I don't believe that at all. She seems quite respectable."

"It's true. But you have to understand that in some cases arranged marriages don't work out. The husband and wife may not develop love and devotion for each other. One solution for wealthy men, and I've heard of it among poor men as well, is to have a keep, or a mistress as you call them in America." His tone was nonchalant, as if having a mistress was the normal way of life.

"I don't call them anything. The topic has never come up for me," she said in a staccato of indignation. It seemed an insult that he should be discussing such a matter with her.

Selvam ignored her tone and continued. "Believe me, in some cases men love and care for their keeps and their keeps' children more than their legitimate families." His tone and the tenseness of muscles around his mouth indicated he wasn't speaking in generalities. Julia felt he had some very specific case in mind. It hit her that he was speaking of them and she looked at him with wide eyes and arched brows, her lips slightly parted.

Selvam turned to her and, seeing her expression, turned his attention back to the road. She had not missed the serious set of his lips, which seemed to affirm her suspicion, before embarrassment forced him to avoid the shock on her face.

Julia grew thoughtful. Selvam was leading her into another layer of this multifaceted land. Just as there were ancient bullock carts alongside modern buses, there was also a world of courtesans, dancers, and mistresses, a tradition of at least nineteen hundred years, if she were to use the date of *Shilappadikaram,* and probably much older. Only this world remained very well hidden, not at all obvious as were the other worlds she had discovered.

But why did Selvam expose her to this darker, immoral side? What were his motives? Julia knew he had no intention of marrying her. Nirmala had made that clear. And yet Selvam continually forced his passion on her. Did he mean to make her his courtesan . . . his keep? Is that why he was having her read *Shilappadikaram?* Is that why he had spoken about modern-day courtesans?

Before she could ponder those thoughts further, the car jerked to a stop. In front of them spread the row of motel rooms of the tourist lodge. The late afternoon sun reflected warmly off the whitewashed wall and the terracotta-tiled roof, and glared back from the ocean on the right side of the building with blinding white light. On the left side the palm thatching of the outdoor restaurant pavilion chuckled in the breeze.

Selvam escorted Julia to a table on the pavilion away from the tourists, both Western and elite Indian, who clustered around the rattan bar or were seated at tables near the bar. Julia sat down in a light green rattan armchair, which swallowed her petite figure. It was positioned in such a way that she could see only Selvam and the beach just behind him. An Indian waiter in a black jacket, looking strangely formal in so informal a setting, deposited large menus in their hands. Julia worried about the exorbitant prices.

Selvam ordered two Limcas, to start. When the waiter had left, he focused his dark eyes on Julia. "So, my father said you were hoping to stay on in India, if you could work it out."

"I'd been thinking that, but . . ."

"I know. The Peace Corps won't continue to support a position at the clinic and the government won't fund another nurse's position."

The waiter returned with two bottles of Limca and two glasses with ice. "You decided what you wish, saar?" asked the waiter.

Julia ordered the fish and chips—half the menu had Western dishes—then Selvam ordered the same. When the waiter left, Selvam remarked, "We are similar in many ways, it is not so? We fit together well."

"Just because we decided on the same item on the menu?" protested Julia.

"It's not that. We discovered the same beach. We dance so well together. And we both like Keats, possibly other poets as well. I also wished those moments in the garden could have gone on forever. It was nice, wasn't it?"

"That seems so long ago, even though it was only a few

days back. I don't think I feel the same now." She had so much more to dislike him for now, she thought silently.

"Exactly, and now . . . Julia, you have brought me such happiness. We are a perfect match. I'm an Americanized Indian and you're an Indianized American, part Indian yourself. We're both caught in between, is it not?"

"Perhaps."

"Don't worry about staying in India. I can arrange it very easily."

"How? What do you mean?"

"I didn't exactly come penniless from America. I had a good practice there for six years, and my salary here will be quite good, for India that is. As you perhaps know, my family owns all the rice land surrounding the clinic. Before the land ceiling laws it was sixty acres. Did you know that?"

"No," said Julia. Sixty acres was quite a lot for such rich land, yielding three crops a year.

"Even now with twelve acres it's more than enough to support a large family in grand style."

"I don't see what all this has to do with me," said Julia a little stiffly.

"It has everything to do with you, Julia. I'll share my income with you. I'll give you whatever you're earning now. More even. Perhaps in time you'll come to feel about me the way I feel about you. But I won't push you."

Was he proposing to make her his mistress? He certainly didn't have marriage in mind. The conversation seemed so strange. Strange because it seemed so normal, so smooth. He hadn't asked her point blank to be his mistress. But then, how would a man make such a proposal? Certainly not in a blunt, direct way. He'd do exactly as Selvam was doing, offer her financial support—the rest would be understood.

Julia couldn't deny that he had very skillfully prepared her to grasp his meaning—talking about keeps and how sometimes men love and provide for their keeps and keeps' children better than their legitimate families, making it sound quite acceptable, if not ideal.

"Really, Selvam, I couldn't take money from you. What would people think?" She tried to control the anger in her voice.

"I don't care what people think," he said emphatically. "You're a good nurse, so I've heard. You could be a great help to me and the clinic in so many ways. Julia, I do need you . . . to be with me."

"Then you're planning to stay?"

"If you stay, I certainly will."

"But I can't take money from you. It would put me in a very awkward position." She chose to pretend she didn't grasp his meaning, about making her his keep. She couldn't tolerate what he was implying. Her heart beat rapidly as her face became frozen.

Selvam saw her worried expression. "Julia, there will be no conditions. You'll owe me nothing. You won't have to cooperate with me on a personal level. Perhaps we could go dancing together and swimming. No Indian woman could be such a good companion for me. But aside from being companions, I wouldn't expect a more mature relationship. I wouldn't expect you to love me, although I do think you'll come to my way in the end. I won't force you. As long as you are with me, that's enough."

"Selvam!" Julia protested, no longer able to control her anger.

"No, don't give me an answer yet," he said stopping her short. "Think about it for some time."

Julia didn't have to think about it. Her mind was clearly

made up. Never, never, never, echoed silently from her depths, but she didn't voice her objections outwardly.

Then she calmed down a bit and mulled over what he had said. He wanted her for his mistress. That much was clear. He wouldn't force her, but that wasn't even the problem. She wondered—and blushed at the thought—if she would have the fortitude herself not to give in to him in the long run, being so close, working with him. His mere presence was enough to distract her completely.

Of course she would have the fortitude, she thought angrily. She would never give in to him. She would never settle for anything less than marriage with any man.

Julia looked at Selvam, wondering what attracted her, despite everything he had said and done to repel her. His strength? His gentleness? He was handsome, but it went beyond that. There was something about him so compelling which made it difficult to refuse him anything. He must have affected Rita in the same way. The only solution, Julia finally thought, was to leave India, to leave Selvam, and to avoid this type of talk altogether.

Selvam changed the topic smoothly and suddenly. They spent the remainder of the evening in irrelevant conversation and large gaps of silence, plus discussing excuses they would use to cover up for their long absence alone together—some medical emergency.

When they returned, he let her go without any sign of the affection they had shared. That tormented her even more than his wicked proposition. And that feeling of torment surprised her.

SEVEN

Dr. Arokiaswamy, dressed in a white medical jacket, looked nervous when he entered Julia's house. "I wish to speak to you before the staff meeting this morning."

Julia had finished dressing in her nurse's uniform and twisting her braided hair into a bun. Her leg felt much better. The ocean water of the previous day had indeed helped very much. She didn't limp anymore, but had to walk just a bit slower than usual.

At the moment the doctor entered, she was applying a light coat of lipstick in front of her mirror. "Yes?" she said, thinking it very unusual for the doctor to come to her house. Even if he wanted to speak to her privately, he could do so at the clinic.

"It is this," he started. "I spoke with my son last night."

Her heart skipped. What had Selvam told him?

"He very much misses America," continued the doctor. "He felt shy, so he asked me if I would consider that you and he work together. At that time I was preparing the new schedule. I have had to revise with Joseph's arrival."

"You want me to work with him?" Julia gasped.

"Of course, only if you are willing to do so, Miss Julia. That is why I wanted to speak to you before the meeting. Joseph himself said he would consider it only if you were willing."

Those words, *only if you were willing*, made Julia frown. It would be easy to refuse Selvam, if he were asking instead of his father. He wouldn't have been able to protest—no, it would be very suspicious if he were to protest her refusal. But he had obviously known that and had sent his father. Now it would look suspicious if *she* refused. Oh, what a craftsman, this Selvam. How he could bend people in any way to fit his desires!

Sufficiently recovered from the shock, Julia said with a tremble, "I don't know, Dr. Arokiaswamy."

The doctor looked dejected. "You see, Joseph does miss America so. I thought if you were to work with him . . . and, as you know, the medical system is a bit different over there. You are the only one familiar with both systems. Well, it did seem like a logical choice."

Julia hesitated, thought, and then replied weakly, "Yes, you're right." She sighed deeply. "I suppose I could at least work with him for a few weeks, until I leave."

"Oh, but Miss Julia, did not I tell you? We may be able to find a way for you to continue here." His face lit up.

Again Julia was shocked. Had Selvam told him of his plan? If so, what would the doctor be thinking? But before her mind could travel down that path, he continued. "It seems Dr. Krishnamurthy has some ideas. He would not tell me as yet, not until he has investigated them."

Julia leaned against the wall and smiled. "That would be wonderful!"

She felt suddenly free from Selvam's manipulations. Her mind whirled around the idea that her dream of staying in India would come true. Might come true, she corrected herself. Dr. Krishnamurthy was just investigating. But it did sound very hopeful.

Dr. Arokiaswamy also smiled and looked a bit giddy with joy. "Then you will work with Joseph?"

"Yes," said Julia with more happiness at the prospect of staying in India than of working with Selvam—which would be quite distracting, she thought, but then brushed the thought aside.

"Then perhaps my son will stay here, if he feels he has an American colleague close by." Dr. Arokiaswamy had his own joy and hope.

The staff meeting was at seven thirty, half an hour before the clinic opened for outpatients. All were present: Dr. Arokiaswamy, Dr. Selvanathan, Raman, Leela, Julia, the three student nurses, and the five other male and female nurses. They all sat on metal folding chairs in a haphazard manner in a small room. Dr. Arokiaswamy stood in front and spoke.

He presented the new schedule, explaining that he put Julia with his son to help orient him to the clinic and into the Indian medical system. It seemed so logical no one even raised an eyebrow. Then he went on to tell about the possibility of Julia staying, that Dr. Krishnamurthy had some ideas which he was investigating.

Julia couldn't help but notice the flash of surprise on Selvam's face. *Touché to you, my dear Selvam,* she thought. The carpet had been pulled out from under his little scheme to make her his keep. Julia beamed with ecstasy over the victory, but her joy was short-lived.

"And there is another possibility," continued Dr. Arokiaswamy, "to improve our clinic yet further. As you know, we very well need two doctors here, and the government has recently agreed to fund another position for a doctor. Joseph may be staying with us. That would solve the problem temporarily at least. But as you well know, I will be retiring within this year and we will need yet another doctor. Now my son, Joseph, has suggested the most brilliant idea—that we should have a lady doctor on our staff."

Immediately everyone nodded or made some noises of affirmation. They all knew that many women were reluctant to go to male doctors. Julia alone froze. The blood drained from her face and her mouth opened slightly as painful thoughts rushed through her mind: His wife. He'd marry a lady doctor and bring her here. It was all a part of his plan from the beginning, just as Nirmala had said.

Julia looked to Selvam, but his face was turned toward Leela. They were whispering. Julia felt as if a door had suddenly slammed in her face. She would never be accepted in this land. She would never be part of a family here.

She was startled by her last thought. Apparently at some deep subconscious level she had actually hoped that Selvam might marry her. She quickly chastised herself for ever entertaining such an idea. How could any decent woman love such a man, much less think of marrying him?

Then she realized that it was her desire to be a part of a family, a perfectly natural desire for an orphan, that had made her hope to marry Selvam, and not—she repeated to herself over and over—any desire for Selvam himself.

"Miss Julia," said Raman, "you look quite pale. Are you ill?"

"Oh, it's nothing," she said quickly. "I guess I'm still a little shook up from my fall the other day."

Raman looked at her with a furrowed brow. Then, coming out of her confusion, she looked around at all the familiar faces, people she had worked with closely for two years. In some ways they were perhaps more intimate than a family, facing problems together, harboring petty resentments at times, but always fostering the solid foundations of affection.

Yes, she did belong here. She did have a family, this clinic family. There was no need to think of marrying such a despicable man as Selvam just to have a family, when she already had one.

Dr. Arokiaswamy, as head of the clinic, closed the meeting by saying that he was so happy his son would be, might be, taking over his position. He concluded with "And all of us on the clinic staff should roll out the red carpet for Joseph and make it impossible for him to leave."

Selvam looked amused and quite satisfied, with his muscular bronze arms folded across his chest and his black hair falling rakishly onto his forehead. He looked ready to accept any red-carpet treatment offered him. Julia thought how arrogant and impossible he was.

For the next week Julia dutifully worked with Selvam. She assisted him during surgery and went with him to village sick calls, which he had taken over from his father. He was an excellent doctor, up-to-date on all the latest research, a very competent diagnostician and surgeon. Julia couldn't help admiring him, even when he sometimes became irritated with her. After all, she came to find out how much a perfectionist he was, and she admired that too.

Before, when they had been together, his attention had been fully on her. Now it shifted to his village patients. Julia became a mere appendage to him, a right arm. He didn't show any sign of affection to her. He remained strictly professional. In a way, she felt glad. She hoped he wouldn't bring up his proposition again. But daily her desire for his embrace and his attention increased, until she couldn't even look at him without a warmth flooding through her.

The thought kept tormenting her that Selvam had lost

interest. She sometimes regretted that she was so aloof, regretted that she didn't express the interest in him she truly felt, an interest which grew out of respect and attraction, and just being together, sharing work and worries, smiles and joys.

Then she would reel with a certain sense of danger. She feared thinking about what Selvam would do if he knew how she felt about him. His size and strength and passion were enough to overpower her.

Before meeting Selvam, she had been independent, strong-willed, able to put off any man with her condescending nurse's stare and professional coolness. Selvam made her knees weak. She gazed fondly at him when he worked, examining the sore throat of a little girl, or sliding his stethoscope over an old man's chest. When his dark, piercing eyes caught hers, she would look away immediately.

No, Selvam must not know of her interest in him. She must remain professionally detached. He was simply a doctor and she, simply a nurse.

Whether Selvam was driven by compassion or perfectionism in his job, Julia didn't know. The effect, the same in either case, was that he didn't stop at single complaints from his patients about a fever, head pain, a sore foot, rashes, or dizziness. He would probe all aspects of the patient's bodily condition, diet, life-style, medical history, and medical heritage. The records she had to keep for each patient overwhelmed her. It certainly went beyond the usual recordkeeping at the clinic—brief records were kept only for inpatients—and even beyond recordkeeping in America. Julia thought it was a little too much.

"Selvam," said Julia one evening as they were driving back from a village near the coast. The sun had just set and the sky had turned dark blue. His name echoed through her mind. She had managed to avoid using it during the previous week. "Don't you think this is too time consuming, this much recordkeeping?"

"You have to understand," he replied in a professional tone, looking straight ahead at the road, "that we're not working with just an arm or a stomach, but with full human beings who have vast physiological heritages."

"I know, but . . ."

"Human life, or any life for that matter, is a continuum throughout a much greater time span than a single life. Birth does not begin life, conception doesn't even begin life. Life was there before, in the parents and grandparents and ancestors. Life is a continuation from the very distant past and will continue even after individual members have died. What we are today is just a small part of this ongoing process which connects us to all other people, even to other species."

"You put it so beautifully, Selvam. With all my classes in biology and human physiology, I never thought of it in such a way."

He continued, not minding her praise, deeply thrust into pondering ideas which he obviously had thought out long before. Julia had merely presented him with an opportunity to express them.

"And people don't live apart from their environment. We're a part of our world and our world is a part of us. What we eat, what we do, what other people and organisms do to us, all these are a part of us, they affect us. And, quite significantly, even intangibles such as ideas are so very important to our ultimate condition. Our behavior is so much influenced by what we believe, whether or not our beliefs are valid."

He turned to Julia and winked, and his professional face

111

changed with a smile. "Now do you understand why I want so much information to be kept in records?"

"Yes," Julia sighed. What else could she say? This was an actively intelligent man she had to deal with. She felt small and weak in his presence, not only physically, but intellectually as well. And both his strength and intellect frightened her a bit. Both could be used against her.

Then she became aware that he had taken a wrong turn and had arrived at the tourist lodge.

"Why did you come here?" she managed to ask through a tightened throat. She suddenly felt unsafe with the man she had come to respect so much.

"I have a craving for fish and chips. *Cinnamma* and Tetru are good cooks, but sometimes I crave Western food."

"Why do you call your mother *cinnamma?*" She had meant to ask the question for some time. *Cinnamma* meant "small mother" and was used for one's "parallel" aunts, like one's mother's younger sister, or father's younger brother's wife, while *athai* applied to "cross" aunts, like one's father's sister, or mother's brother's wife.

"Because," said Selvam pedantically, "she's my father's second wife. My mother died when I was eight."

Now Selvam's family began to make sense to Julia. Mrs. Arokiaswamy was only in her forties, too young to be Selvam's mother. And perhaps the strain between Selvam and his father came from the remarriage. But then, Selvam liked his *cinnamma.* Julia's mind skipped to wondering about his real mother. She remembered the picture in his house, the one which had a fresh garland of jasmine after he had returned.

"Then that picture near the niche for the Holy Family, the one of the young woman, is that your mother?"

112

"Yes," replied Selvam. "She was only twenty-nine when she died."

"I always wondered, but never asked. And then when you came from America, it was you who put the garland on the picture."

"Do you find our customs strange?" he asked distantly, as if he were some travel guide rather than the man who had been working so closely with her, or the man who had kissed her—it seemed so long ago—on the beach.

"No, of course not," she said, hurt that he would even suggest such a thing. "I love Indian customs. I think they're so gracious, showing such sensitivity and affection."

"I'm glad you do, Miss Julia," he said warmly. "Now let's go and eat."

Julia was again hurt that he had called her "Miss" when they were alone. In such subtle ways he tormented her and twisted her emotions.

They went to their same rattan table. The waiter came and lit the candle for them. It took several tries as the breeze playfully put out the match. Finally the candle caught, but held Julia on the edge of her seat throughout dinner, as the flame flickered wildly, threatening to go out.

After eating, Selvam took her hand and led her into the darkness of the beach. They had left their shoes and sandals on the pavilion. The warm sand felt good as they walked slowly, and Selvam's hand sent electriclike pulses through Julia. Then Selvam broke the silence.

"I brought you here for a reason."

Her heart jumped. "What?" she asked as if it were a matter of minor importance and not something affecting her whole life.

"Remember when we were here before? I told you I wanted you to stay. I'd share my salary with you—no

113

strings attached unless you thought otherwise. I didn't want to push you. I thought if you knew me better . . . That's why I had my father put us together. I haven't pushed you, have I?"

"No," admitted Julia. She smiled because he had not lost interest in her. But her smile rapidly faded as the dread of what he was leading up to shook her senses.

"Well, my dear Julia, I would like to know what you've decided. I must warn you, though, I don't think I can go on simply as your platonic friend. I hope you've also come to my way of thinking. I must know now if you truly love me."

Julia sighed. He was making the same wretched proposal. This time, however, he was more obvious about his intentions of making her his keep. She couldn't forget that he had told his parents he wanted to marry a woman doctor and was behind the idea of bringing a woman doctor to the clinic.

A week ago she was about to answer him with an emphatic "No!" and possibly would have thrown in some curse words as well—despite promising Dr. Arokiaswamy she'd be kind to him. Now she couldn't easily say no. She had come to love him and wanted to be with him, and yet she could never accept his proposition.

"Selvam," she started slowly, "the last time you asked me to wait before I replied, and now I'm more confused than ever. Nothing's been settled in my mind. Please, I must ask for a favor."

"Anything. Whatever I have, it's all for you." He spoke with a deep voice, full of affection, as if he would give her all the stars in the sky.

Julia was not deceived. She knew exactly what he was offering, and it wasn't much to her way of thinking. But it was something, a chance to be with him, to be loved by

114

him. Finally she said, "I'd like to have more time to think it over."

"More time?" he shouted with surprise. "You'll be leaving in twelve days. Nirmala's marriage is this Friday. And I have other important matters to attend to. I'd give you all the time in the world. I know we haven't known each other very long. But there just isn't any time to give."

"I must have more time." Her voice was firm, though she spoke haltingly. "I cannot give you an answer now, because I do not have an answer."

"Julia, you're holding me in such suspense." He gently gripped her shoulders and sighed. His eyes searched hers in the semi-darkness. "I knew about you from the letters. I knew you were a fine person. But I never expected to fall in love with you, so quickly and so completely. I couldn't bear to lose you now."

He studied her face and throat, lighted partly by the yellow light of the distant pavilion, and partly by the silver-blue light of the almost full moon.

"Had we but world enough, and time,
This coyness, lady, were no crime."

Julia recognized the poem, Andrew Marvell's "To His Coy Mistress." She shuddered and cried out, "Selvam, please!"

"All right," he said in defeat, "take the time you need."

They continued farther down the beach, and as they walked, he asked, "What is it, Julia?"

"What?" she asked.

"What are you running away from?"

Julia stopped and turned toward him. "What do you mean?"

Selvam also stopped and caught her gaze with his intent black eyes. "Why do you want to stay at the clinic?"

"I'm not running away from anything," she said, her voice full of indignation. "I'm a nurse. I want to help. And they need me at the clinic."

"They like you, Julia, and they could always use extra help, but they can manage without you. They don't really need you as desperately as you think they do. So why are you hiding from the world?"

She looked up at his face, her eyes blazing with anger. "I'm not hiding and I'm not running away!" But his words haunted her because they seemed to hold a spark of truth.

Selvam grasped her arms. "You're afraid of becoming involved, aren't you? Perhaps because you lost your parents."

"Oh, I didn't know you were a psychiatrist," she said sharply.

His grip tightened on her arms. "You're afraid of becoming involved with a man. Is that it?"

"Yes," she shouted, thinking of the type of involvement he was referring to, love without any hope of marriage. And she had even been afraid of marriage, or any commitment before. He was right. But now he was totally wrong. For the first time in her life she did want to become involved. She wanted more than anything else to love him, and to be loved by him, but not in the way he intended. Perhaps in America she would have given it consideration —didn't they say it was the relationship that counted, not the marriage license? But in India it was all so degrading. She lowered her head and started to cry. "No," she said through her tears, "I'm not afraid. It's just that . . . oh, I don't know."

Selvam released his grip and encircled her with his

arms, sheltering her against his shoulder. "Don't cry, Julia. You're so fragile, so tender. I didn't mean to . . ." He stroked her head.

When Julia stopped crying he released her, but kept his hands on her shoulders. "I said that you weren't really needed at the clinic, but Julia, I need you. I need you very much."

He kissed her on the forehead, then pulled her into his arms. "I love you, Julia." His lips met hers and his kiss continued, seeming to stretch into infinity. Julia melted in his arms. He held her so tenderly, sensuously teasing her with his lips, that she slid her arms around his neck and pulled him closer, demanding his more passionate kisses, until he was kissing her fiercely. She wanted it to go on forever.

When he finally pulled back, leaving her breathless, he smiled and said, "Just a sample of more to come, should you decide to stay with me."

"I don't think we should . . . I don't think it's wise for us to kiss." She trembled, fearing that much more of his lovemaking would lead her to the point at which she would agree to be his mistress.

He laughed out loud. "You are such a mysterious little creature, so womanly and yet so childlike. Come, let's go home now."

They went back to the tourist lodge without any further conversation. In the car Selvam took a drag on his cigarette and exhaled. Then he looked down at her with a gleam in his eyes. "Someday we'll come here and take a room, hmm? I know what you want, but you perhaps need more time to know it yourself."

Heat flashed through Julia's face. "You're so infuriating, Selvam!"

He laughed, and she smiled, realizing how she had come

to love even his devilish teasing. But it wasn't really teasing, she thought, and became serious.

Julia had not only been pondering Selvam's proposition for the past week, she had also been waiting for news from Dr. Krishnamurthy. So when he and Dr. Arokiaswamy drove up to her house the next day around tiffin time, Julia became very excited.

"Miss Julia," said the stout old Dr. Krishnamurthy as he entered Julia's small living room. "I am glad to say we have good news. There is a way you can stay with us."

"Oh, thank you so much. . . . Please come and sit down. I've just prepared coffee. Please."

The two doctors sat down while Julia went to the small kitchen and brought back two tumblers of coffee. She handed them to them and sat down on a stool, perching expectantly while her brown eyes glimmered back and forth between the two doctors. "What is it?" she asked, unable to contain her excitement.

"Well . . ." Dr. Krishnamurthy looked at Dr. Arokiaswamy and then at Julia. "It is a slightly complicated situation, but I have talked with Dr. Arokiaswamy and he thinks it is an excellent idea."

Julia felt a little surprised that they weren't telling her directly.

"Miss Julia," said Dr. Arokiaswamy, "it really depends on you now, whether or not you would be agreeable."

"Yes?" she said slowly.

"Well, let me ask," said Dr. Arokiaswamy. "Would you consider marriage to an Indian man?" His face muscles contracted slightly with embarrassment.

Julia's cheeks reddened with embarrassment also. She thought, closing her eyes, that they were arranging for her to marry Selvam. She answered softly, trying to keep the jubilant ring out of her voice, "Yes, I'd consider it."

"I thought you might," said Dr. Krishnamurthy, "so I contacted Mr. Kumarswamy of Udaipuram. You have met him. He speaks fondly of you. I suggested if he would marry you. He is a modern boy. He understands much about Western customs, and he was very agreeable. As it turns out, he had even thought of the idea himself, but was too shy to tell anyone."

Julia lowered her gaze to the green-gray cement floor and sighed. *Mr. Kumarswamy*, she thought. How could she even consider marrying him? She loved Selvam. She always would, even if it meant never marrying him. But then there was Kumarswamy who wanted to marry her. He offered her something Selvam had never offered, a home, a decent family life.

She had so hoped Dr. Krishnamurthy would have come up with a good solution. Now she felt mercilessly boxed in, surrounded by unacceptable choices, enveloped just as the extreme heat of the season enveloped her, offering no respite.

"Of course," continued Dr. Krishnamurthy, "there are some things you must know about Mr. Kumarswamy, before you consider the proposal. He is a very wealthy businessman in my town, and well liked by most people. However, I have to inform you that his mother was a famous dancer and she never married."

"Yes, I know, Selvam . . ." She caught herself, but not in time. Both doctors looked at her in astonishment.

"Dr. Selvanathan," started Dr. Arokiaswamy, "told you?"

"Yes," she said casually, having regained her composure. "He made a house call on Mr. Kumarswamy's mother, and on our way back he happened to mention

. . ." She spoke as if it were the most natural, logical thing for Selvam to talk about, but the two doctors didn't seem to think so.

Dr. Arokiaswamy interrupted, "What else did he tell you?"

"Nothing else. See, we were discussing *Shilappadikaram* and he was just giving an example . . ." Julia wondered what else there was to know.

The doctors seemed satisfied with her answer and Dr. Krishnamurthy spoke. "Then since you know about the situation, the benefits, and shall we say, the other side, you will be able to come to some decision."

"Would he wish for me to continue working?" Julia didn't know why she was asking that, as if she actually contemplated the marriage.

"Oh, yes, by all means, if you wish to do so. But he would wish that your work load be less, and that half the time you could work in Udaipuram with me. We, all three of us, Dr. Arokiaswamy, Mr. Kumarswamy, and myself, were very much in agreement with the idea. So now it is for you to decide."

Julia knew she should say no in all fairness to the doctors and to the man who wanted to marry her, but in a new state of confusion, she said that she would need a few days to think it over. They said they very well understood and left.

Late that night, around ten thirty, shortly after the dinner hour, Julia stood in front of her mirror, brushing her sable hair to a sheen. She wore a thin, sleeveless sundress which made her feel comfortable in the warmth of the night. Suddenly but quietly Selvam burst through the door, his face hardened with anger, every muscle in his body tense. His red and orange *kaili* was doubled up to above his knees, revealing his sinuous legs. Only the two bottom buttons of his white shirt were fastened.

He grabbed Julia's arm and she started to protest, but he covered her mouth with his hand. He whispered angrily, "Keep quiet. Do you want Ramanathan and Leela to know I'm here?"

She shook her head no, and he released his hand from her mouth, but held her arm even tighter. Then he took the brush away from her and put it down on the shelf just below the mirror. Squeezing her upper arm so hard that it throbbed with pain, he forced her out of the house. Her flowing hair shimmered with the vibrations of her protesting movements.

Quietly he led her away from the compound down the road until they reached a distance where their voices could not be heard back at the clinic. They stood on the road, drenched in moonlight. Julia could see the anger in his eyes.

"What is this?" he asked roughly. "*Appa* just now told me at dinner . . . I couldn't finish eating. . . ."

"Selvam, you're hurting my arm."

"Hurting your arm! How do you think I felt when my father told me that marriage was being arranged between you and that . . . that Kumarswamy? I have gravely misjudged you!" His lips formed a tight line.

"I didn't say I'd definitely marry him," Julia protested indignantly.

"You said you'd consider it," he shouted.

Julia bowed her head and her hair fell forward onto her cheeks. She felt guilty, but guilty of what? How could she have betrayed Selvam, if there was no relationship between them? What was her relationship with Selvam anyway? A few kisses, a little male-female interest? That was certainly not enough to make it a crime. And yet here was Selvam in all his possessive arrogance, outraged because she had considered marrying another man—when he himself had not offered her as much.

Selvam released her arm and said a bit more gently, "I thought you felt something special for me. Apparently I was wrong."

"Selvam, I do feel something special for you." She lightly touched his arm. "But I have a right to consider my own happiness. I want to get married and have a family. I never thought I'd want that, but I do. I . . . I couldn't settle for anything less." She was indirectly giving him his answer, and she had surprised even herself, because only at this moment, in her own heart, did she completely reject the proposition to be his keep.

"Then does that mean you love this man?"

"No, I don't," she said truthfully.

"Then why, Julia? How could you even consider marrying a man you don't love?" He was angry and hurt.

"But I told you. . . ." She started to explain the real point between her and Selvam—that she just couldn't have a relationship without marriage.

"Come to me, Julia," he interrupted. He pulled her small hand up to his chest. His heart pounded strongly. He pulled her into his arms. All at once his lips were on hers, fiercely demanding her response. One arm held her tightly, crumpling her body against his, while his free hand rubbed her bare arm.

Julia hesitated at first, until her whole body reverberated with a passion she had only felt when he had kissed her before, surpassing that passion now. She lifted her arms around his neck and kissed him back feverishly, until the world fell away and her knees weakened. He supported her in his embrace, welding her soft body to his.

Selvam's hungry lips traveled over her cheeks and down her throat. Julia moaned softly with passion, willing to be whatever Selvam wanted, willing at this moment to accept his proposition, to be his mistress if that were all she could be to him.

Then he pushed her away, gripping her shoulders because she seemed about to fall.

"See, Julia, how you drive me mad." His voice again became angry. "You're like a drug to me and I'm addicted. I love you! Don't you realize that?"

"And what about me?" she cried in a tight, hoarse voice. "You torment me and torment me."

"Then why, Julia?" he shouted. "Why are you even considering to marry that Kumarswamy? How can you do this to me?" His face contorted with anguish. "The son of my father's keep!"

Julia gasped. Dr. Arokiaswamy? How could it be? He was the epitome of goodness and decency. He was a model to emulate. His mistress? But before Julia could speak, the bells from a bullock cart jingled down the road. The sound quickly crescendoed as the cart approached them.

"Joseph?" called the female rider inside the quonset-shaped roof of the cart. Then in Tamil she told the driver to stop.

"*Athai,* it is you?" called Selvam. Then he whispered to Julia, "My mother's brother's wife. Rita's mother. She's come to help with Nirmala's wedding."

Julia felt a rush of shame. Here she stood out on a road late at night, with a man, her hair streaming down wildly. Would she have ever accepted Selvam's proposition to be his keep? No matter. Whatever else would happen, she was now a marked woman. She knew very well how Indian women thrived on daily gossip, and would turn even the most minor incident into a scandal.

At the insistence of Rita's mother, Julia and Selvam climbed into the cart and rode back to the clinic. Selvam let Julia out at her home, offering a quiet and distant, "Good night."

EIGHT

Dr. Arokiaswamy closed the clinic for the rest of the week, except for emergency cases and the twelve inpatients. Nirmala's marriage celebration was to start the next day, Thursday, with *nalangu,* the ceremony for blessing the bride and groom. Then the wedding mass would be on Friday.

Relatives from all over Tamil Nadu and even some from out-of-state arrived to help with the wedding. The guest house, a large, two-story house within the clinic compound, which had been the doctor's quarters before Dr. Arokiaswamy had built his own house, was prepared for the groom's party.

The early morning sun had just climbed above the feathery coconut trees when Julia, in white slacks and a rust-colored blouse, wandered up to Dr. Arokiaswamy's house. Bare-chested workmen in faded *kailis* were busy constructing the large marriage *pandal* of bamboo poles and palm fronds, attached to the house and extending over the driveway.

Julia worried about the garden plants. Some were already being trampled. The marriage would bring devastation to the weaker plants near the *pandal,* the pink roses and lacy ice plants with purple flowers that opened only in the morning shade, and then closed up for the rest of the day.

No one seemed to notice Julia as she stood outside the low compound wall of the doctor's house, no one except two small girls who stopped playing and stared with wide black eyes and soft mouths. Their matching pink dresses contrasted beautifully with their black, cropped hair.

Julia smiled at them. The older one, about eight, smiled back, while the younger one, about five, stood awed. Then Selvam came through the bougainvillea arcade of the gate. His deep voice made Julia's blood warm.

"My nieces seem as enthralled with you as I am."

"Mama!" squealed the girls, running toward him.

They must be his father's brother's granddaughters, or some such relation, thought Julia. They couldn't be his sister's daughters since Nirmala wasn't even married yet, and they had referred to Selvam as *mama,* their "cross" uncle, their classificatory mother's brother.

Julia saw the gleam of the morning sun in Selvam's eyes as he gazed down at her. His smile suggested a familiarity which made Julia lower her eyes, and his blue shirt, the same one he had worn at the dance in Madras, made her blush as she thought about how it felt to dance with him.

The little girls ran up to Selvam. Each grabbed one of his hands and he squatted down to them.

"Who is the pretty lady?" the older one asked in Tamil.

"Oh, she is my girl friend," said Selvam.

The girls broke out giggling, then the younger one protested, "But you promised to marry me, *mama.* Last night you said."

Selvam laughed at the earnest little five-year old. "So I did. You are right. Well, then I must marry all three of you."

The girls again giggled and he hugged them both, while the younger one pulled at his hair.

"And you must marry Rita too," said Julia. She suddenly regretted bringing up the topic at this time and place, especially after she had been putting it off in deference to Dr. Arokiaswamy's wishes. She also feared that Selvam would admit his true intention of marrying a well-educated, rich woman. It was a topic she didn't want to face.

Selvam stood up and told the girls to go help their mother. He looked at Julia seriously as the girls ran away. "Just because Rita's my cousin, it doesn't mean I have to marry her. I have no intention of marrying her. Is that why you've been so hesitant about me, Julia?"

"No, I know you don't intend to marry Rita," she said softly, stopping herself from adding the rest of what Nirmala had told her.

Selvam stepped closer to her, as if about to grasp her arms. Julia stepped back and asked, "Did you tell your aunt that I . . . I was your girl friend?" She shuddered to think about all the gossip that would be going around the house, and Dr. Arokiaswamy's shock at hearing how Rita's mother had found them on the road together the previous night.

A mischievous smile crossed Selvam's face. "I was tempted to do so, but I told *athai* that I'd gone for a walk and that apparently you'd also gone for a walk, and that we had just met when she drove up. She made some comment about you having that much courage to walk alone at night, but nothing else came of it."

Julia sighed with immediate relief. "Thank you," she whispered.

"And now," he said a bit harshly, "what about that Kumarswamy?"

127

Julia blushed. She had her own question to ask. All night she had been tormented, unable to sleep thinking about Selvam's accusation that Kavitha was Dr. Arokiaswamy's mistress. She had to know the truth.

Before she could counter Selvam's question with her own question, Leela came up the path. "Joseph and Julia. You are always together, at work and now. If I need to find one, then I simply look for the other. There is something between you, I can see it."

Both Selvam and Julia froze with embarrassment. "*Akka,*" said Selvam, calling Leela his older sister out of respect and affection, "you're imagining too much."

"Am I?" she asked pointedly to Selvam, then she looked at Julia and said, "I wanted to talk to both of you."

"I was just leaving," said Selvam. "Already I'm late." He walked toward the car which had been parked on the road. "I'll be back tomorrow," he called back. "Tell *appa.*"

Before Leela could protest, he was in the car and driving away. "That Joseph," Leela said. "With his sister's wedding starting tomorrow he is going off somewhere. He did not even tell his father." She turned to Julia. "Come, let us go to my house and talk. We will come later for helping with wedding preparations."

At Leela's home, Julia sat down rather shamefacedly, thinking that Leela would scold her, as her tone had indicated, but instead Leela's face and voice softened as she sat down and leaned forward.

"I was so hoping you and Joseph would find love together, and I am so happy to see that you have."

"What are you saying?" Julia interrupted.

Leela smiled. "I have known from the start. It is obvious, the way he looks at you, and how you look at him."

"My God! Do others think . . ."

"No, I am sure no one suspects. Only I can guess what is truly in your heart and Joseph's. He used to confide in me as a child, even before his mother died. I took care of him. His mother was always very sickly. And I knew before either of you knew or even met what a good match you would be for Joseph."

She paused and searched Julia's silent face. "I wrote to him in America. For two years I have written about you, the beautiful girl, so quiet and sweet. I wrote how very well you have adjusted to India. He was interested in you before he saw you. He wrote back asking about you. And I also tried to tell you about him, is it not?"

Julia felt embarrassed. She didn't want to hear any more about how Leela had schemed to bring them together, especially now that their relationship seemed doomed. Besides, Julia burned with her own question. "Is Kavitha Dr. Arokiaswamy's keep?"

"Who told you such a thing?" Leela sat straight, pulling away from Julia.

"Dr. Selvanathan," said Julia, feeling as always a bit odd using his formal title.

"*Appa-di-o!* How could he know that? He was just a child." Leela shook her head and Julia saw the torment on her face. "It must have been his mother. Or maybe he overheard their arguments. All these years we thought the resentment was because his father had been away when his mother died. Now it is clear. But of course . . ."

Julia looked away, wishing she could shut her ears against the truth. Dr. Arokiaswamy never raised his voice, never spoke an unkind word, and now he appeared to be some kind of villain, whereas Selvam came off looking like some wronged hero—arrogant and domineering Selvam, who in fact had the similar villainous intentions of his father. Didn't he also want a keep?

129

Leela sensed Julia's thought, at least the first part of it, as a well-seasoned navigator can read the sea and stars.

"Julia, do not think wrong of Dr. Arokiaswamy. It is understandable. Joseph's mother was very sickly. Dr. Arokiaswamy's mother was alive then. She constantly complained about her daughter-in-law. Both the doctor and his wife suffered greatly. Then during the delivery of Joseph she nearly died. The doctor was much worried. He loved his wife so very much."

Leela paused for a moment, trying to find a way to phrase her next words. "The doctor knew that she would never survive another childbirth. That is when he built their very grand house. He put his wife and son there with plenty of servants. He and his mother remained in the doctor's quarters. I think they never shared the same bed again, not after Joseph's birth."

Julia felt the anguish in Leela's voice, the tightening of the throat. Leela gulped some air before continuing. "It was after many years that the doctor took Kavitha as his keep. I did not blame Dr. Arokiaswamy. He had been very miserable and his mother continued to split him and his wife. Kavitha made the doctor happy for a short while only. But some way Mrs. Arokiaswamy came to know and she could never accept it. There were arguments.

"Then one day Joseph came running to me at the clinic. He was just a little boy of eight years. He was crying and crying. He told me his mother was very ill. Of course I rushed to see her. Dr. Arokiaswamy was out of the clinic at the time."

Leela paused and again inhaled deeply, as if out of breath. Julia pictured Selvam as a boy crying for his sick mother and her heart swelled with sorrow for him as she waited expectantly for Leela to go on with the story.

"The doctor was with his Kavitha. Oh, Julia, there was

nothing he could have done anyway. She died shortly after I arrived, and poor little Joseph, he was calling for his father. 'Appa will make her well. Appa will make her well,' he cried. I told him, 'No, no, your mother is dead.' He became very silent then, as if his tender little heart was somehow becoming hard against the pain.

"Oh, Julia, he must know the whole story, about his mother's sickness and that she couldn't have more children. He must be told how much his father really did love his mother and that after her death he never again went to Kavitha, except as a doctor. He must not go on with such bad feelings for his father without knowing the complete story. I must tell him."

Julia nodded her head. "Yes, he should know. It also hurts me to see the tension between Dr. Arokiaswamy and Selvam."

"So, you call him Selvam, just as his mother did." Leela smiled sadly at Julia. "And I can see that you do love him, the way you speak his name, so tenderly."

"Oh, yes," said Julia desperately, a bit startled by her admission. "I do love him. I love him so much, it hurts." By the passion in her voice she longed to reach out to him, to tell him also of her love. Then she sighed and added, "But he must never know. Leela, you mustn't let him know."

"Why? He does love you, is it not?"

"Yes, he does love me in his own way. But we're not right for each other."

"No, Julia. Do not say that. I know you both very well. I know your Selvam, perhaps better than you do. You *are* right for each other."

"Leela, you don't understand." Julia's voice became shrill with anguish. "He doesn't want to marry me. He wants to make me his *keep!*"

"No!" Leela's voice burst, filling the whole room. "That cannot be. He told you that?"

"He didn't say it directly, but he made it very clear to me:" Her eyes focused hopelessly on the cement floor.

"But if he did not tell you directly, how can you know? I am sure you are wrong. Joseph is a good boy. He would not be that way."

"He is not a good boy!" Julia became angry. "He told his family that he would marry only a girl from his caste, well educated, preferably a lady doctor. He wants a huge dowry. Nirmala told me. And he did make it quite clear that he wants me as his keep. He has never mentioned marriage to me. He only said he'd support me financially."

"But that does not sound like Joseph. It is just so hard to believe."

"Just as hard as it was for me to believe that Dr. Aro-kiaswamy had a keep," said Julia, as if offering more evidence for her case.

"Maybe I just do not understand men very well. My husband is so good. Perhaps I have been judging Joseph by my husband's standards. Oh, but this is just so terrible what you tell me."

"And it's even more terrible," said Julia, her eyes glistening with tears, "because I love him so much. I know he's a scoundrel, but I can't bear the thought of being away from him. I don't want to be his mistress, but there doesn't seem to be any alternative. I just don't know what to do." Julia started crying softly and Leela came over to her and held her head against her shoulder, patting her on the back.

"I think it is my fault. What have I done?" asked Leela sadly.

Julia controlled her crying. "We would've fallen in love anyway. I just don't know whether I'm happy or miserable. I don't know whether to leave him or stay and take whatever he offers."

Leela pulled back from Julia. She held her shoulders and looked at her earnestly. "Julia, you must go. It will only lead to ruin if you stay. But you know I do not wish you to go."

Again Leela hugged Julia, this time strongly. "You must go, Julia," she repeated. Her voice held a tone of despair.

"Yes, I know," said Julia soberly. Then she pulled back a little from Leela. "But please promise me one thing."

"What is it?"

"Selvam must not know that I love him. If he finds out, I don't think he'll let me leave. He has a certain power over me. I think he could make me stay, and on his terms. I feel it. I'm not as strong a person as I thought I was."

"Of course. It is understandable. He has always been very commanding. Your secret is safe with me."

Julia and Leela were not quite in jovial spirits when they went to help with the marriage preparations. Julia felt glad she could take on the task of stitching lace to the wedding veil on Mrs. Arokiaswamy's treadle sewing machine. In that way she faced the yellow wall in the guest room just off the main hall, and no one could see the pain in her eyes.

The conversation with Leela had brought her sharply back to reality. She knew she must leave India, and the idea hurt her more now than ever. Selvam had come into her life and upset everything, her plans, her heart, her very existence. He had introduced her to a new world, the world of love. This world would be especially difficult to leave. Just knowing Selvam was away from the clinic gave her a hard, gnawing sensation in her stomach and a tightness in her throat. Leaving him for good would be most difficult.

Nirmala entered the room and looked at the veil as it slid smoothly under the foot of the sewing machine.

"Julia, Leela said you were with Joe *annan* when he left. Did he tell you where he was going?" asked Nirmala.

Without looking up Julia said, "No, he didn't say. He just took off."

"Was he angry when he left?"

Julia now stopped her sewing and turned to look up at Nirmala. A worried face met a worried face. "No, he wasn't angry. He seemed rather abrupt, but he's always that way."

Nirmala gave a sigh of relief. Julia became perplexed and asked, "Why do you think he was angry?"

"Oh, it is nothing. Last night again the topic of his marriage to Rita came up after Rita's mother arrived. It was very embarrassing. He had to explain to her how he wanted to marry a lady doctor."

Julia felt as if she had been freshly struck with some dreadful news, as if she had not already known Selvam's plans. She closed her eyes and felt her heart sink.

Nirmala continued, "Of course he was very kindly to *athai* and told that he would help with Rita's marriage. But *athai* was not satisfied. She brought up all past family matters. Everyone became upset. Then *athai* started accusing *annan* of . . . well, I really should not tell you this, but she accused him of having some relationship with you."

Julia's face turned pale and she interrupted with a quavering voice, "That's completely absurd. I just went for a walk last night and . . ."

Overlapping her protest, Nirmala interrupted with "I

know. *Annan* explained it all. He said that you meant absolutely nothing to him."

Though Julia for the world didn't want anyone to know about Selvam and herself, Nirmala's last words cut her deeply with pain. The same man who had shown so much passion to her and had told her with complete sincerity how much he loved her, had a few minutes later told others how she meant absolutely nothing to him.

Julia asked Nirmala for the exact words Selvam had used and listened to the same harsh words again. She sighed and asked lazily, "And then what happened?"

"Everyone accepted what Joe *annan* said. Of course it is very understandable that a medical doctor would want to marry a medical doctor, and we all knew *athai* was just angry. That's why she said about you and *annan*. But *appa* . . ."

Nirmala hesitated and Julia waited with growing dread for her to continue. "It is this way. I went to bed shortly after that. So did everyone else. It was well after midnight. But my room is just above this guest room—Joe *annan*'s room for now—and I could barely hear *appa* speaking with *annan*.

"He asked if it was true about something between you and *annan*. Again *annan* denied it, but he spoke very unkindly to *appa* saying something that because *appa* had done so many things in his life, he had no right to question Joe *annan*'s life. I do not know what he meant.

"Then *appa* said that *annan* perhaps should be married very soon, so his mind would not wander in some wrong direction. He said he must find a suitable match for Joe *annan* as soon as my marriage is completed, and then have Joe *annan*'s wedding before *adi masam,* if possible.

"Joe *annan* agreed with that. You know *adi* is the Tamil

month after the marriage season. It is inauspicious for marriages then."

Julia nodded and thought that *adi masam* was only a little more than a month away. Selvam would be sharing the marriage bed with another woman in less than a month. The future was becoming a painful reality very quickly.

Before Nirmala could read Julia's expression, Mrs. Arokiaswamy came and reminded them that there were many things to be done. She wanted Julia to stitch a new cloth for the niche, and Nirmala would have to start sorting through all her belongings. There wouldn't be much time to pack after the wedding.

Nirmala's face immediately changed. "*Amma,* I do not want to leave you and *appa,*" she cried in Tamil, torn by her own dilemma. Her mood blended with Julia's and Mrs. Arokiaswamy, holding back her own emotions, set about putting Nirmala and Julia to work that day and the next.

Selvam had not returned when the women held their first ceremony late in the afternoon, the day before the wedding. Mrs. Arokiaswamy, Rita's mother, and two other female relatives joined together in the ceremony of erecting the *muhurtham* pole, the most easterly pole of the *pandal.*

Nirmala lagged behind to ask Julia if her brother had returned. When Julia said she hadn't seen him, Nirmala went to join the other women, her lips slightly turned down with disappointment.

Julia looked on as the five women knelt on the sandy ground while a bare-chested man in a *kaili* placed a long, thick bamboo pole in a hole. After that the man took a coconut in his hand and juggled it to position the angle.

With one swift stroke of his large machete he broke the coconut in half, allowing the water to fall at the base of the pole.

The women took a steel plate with small steel bowls of water, turmeric powder, *kungamam,* sandalwood powder, and turmeric-coated rice. They marked the pole with the powders and water, and sprinkled rice at the base; then the man filled up the hole. The women knelt again and Mrs. Arokiaswamy led them in some Christian prayers.

As the women finished the ceremony, rising up and dusting off their silk saris, Siva came to inform them that the groom's party had arrived at the guest house.

By the time the guests on both sides received tiffin, and more and more guests were streaming in, the atmosphere of the clinic and doctor's house had become strangely electric. People milled about everywhere, women in bright silk saris, teen-age girls in their traditional half saris and full-length silk skirts, men in pants and shirts, some in white *dhotis,* some in full Western dress suit, and children in frocks and shorts, playing tag in and out among the adults. Soon the sky darkened, but the clinic area remained luminous with the tube lights and alive with all the people.

Julia, dressed in a silk suit, had shown the groom's maternal uncle, his wife, and three small daughters to her house—she was doubling up with Leela and Raman for the night—when the loud skirl of the Tamil flute suddenly pierced through the whole clinic, sending lumps of sensation to her chest and throat. All stood silent and attentive while the flute marked the auspicious moment.

"The marriage has begun," said Leela, standing next to Julia in their common yard.

As the crude leather drums and cymbals in the five-man band joined in orchestration with the complex lilt of the

137

flute, tears came to Julia's eyes. The once little girl, Nirmala, had entered womanhood and now stood at the threshold of marriage. Julia felt chills gliding along her arms, as if Selvam had touched her. She hoped he had returned. How irresponsible of him to have dashed away, she thought.

Soon after the music had started, a group of women from the groom's side went to Dr. Arokiaswamy's house, then brought Nirmala and her female relatives back in a grand procession to the guest house. Julia and Leela joined in to watch the *nalangu* ceremony.

Because only married women and close family men blessed the bride and groom and because Julia was not a relative, she stood at the entrance of the guest house, while Leela went in through the crowd to be close to Nirmala. Julia contented herself by imagining how it would be if she were the bride and Selvam the groom.

At the far end of the main hall, Nirmala sat in a teak armchair. Her mother and the closest relatives hovered around her. Among the ample, sari-clad women, Julia could see flashes of Nirmala and tried to imagine herself someday in Nirmala's place, with rhinestones decorating her hairline and running down her part, with layers of gold necklaces and bangles, with an abundance of jasmine blossoms covering the back of her head and braid, and with small sandalwood paste dots on her forehead—eyes to keep away evil eyes at this most important time of her life.

The women and closest male relatives blessed Nirmala by smearing *kungamam* on her forehead, turmeric and sandalwood paste on the back's of her hands, and by sprinkling her with saffron-coated rice, jasmine petals, and rose water. Julia's radiant smile matched Nirmala's as she soared through her own fantasy world.

Then she saw Selvam in a raw silk shirt and black pants. He was blessing Nirmala according to custom, after which he leaned over and kissed her on the cheek. Julia's heart skipped and her body became numb. Selvam's presence brought with it a reality that made her ache to be with him, to share his life, and at the same time it brought the reality that such a desire could never be fulfilled.

A short, immense woman jostled her for a better view, and Julia shrank back. Without willpower to stand her ground, she was pushed out onto the veranda into the uncomfortable position between the crowd of women in front and the men outside, who were trying to see the ceremony through the door and windows.

Time seemed to stand still. Julia could no longer see Nirmala, who would soon be replaced by the groom in the ceremony. She had a vague desire to escape from the pressing crowd, but instead stood almost dazed.

It became clearer to her than ever before that she didn't belong in the women's world. The women inside knew it, and now she knew it, really knew it, and it hurt. The crowd had a dizzying effect on her. Time became eternity.

Then the presence of a man close behind Julia jolted her back to reality. She felt his breath on her neck—or she thought it was his breath. A warm breeze wove in and out of the crowd, a hot stuffy breeze. It could have been that.

As an electric shock, she felt the man's hands grasp her arms and his body press against hers, as if to push her out of the way, or perhaps to take advantage of touching her. It sometimes happened, men touching women in large crowds. She decided to tell him quietly, with gritted teeth, to move away from her. She turned, ready to flash her hot temper at him, and saw Selvam smiling down at her with such tenderness in his face.

She closed her eyes, and her knees buckled. Selvam

139

grabbed her before she could fall. Then he led her away from the crowd to the courtyard of the clinic. The kitchen in the nearby commissary buzzed with chatter and cast a yellow light into the courtyard. Dinner would soon be served for the guests. He moved her into a corner where they could be alone and unseen.

Julia half-expected Selvam to take her in his arms and kiss her, but instead he looked at her coolly.

"Well, what about Kumarswamy?"

"Kumarswamy?" Julia shuddered from Selvam's abruptness. "I informed Dr. Krishnamurthy today that I couldn't accept the offer." She looked straight at him with her own cool stare. "You *know* I never intended to marry him."

"No, I didn't know. You never told me. You only said you didn't love him."

"But I could never marry anyone if I weren't in love with him."

"Many people get married without being in love," he said.

"But I couldn't."

"Then do you love me, Julia?" he asked in a serious tone, edged with tenderness.

Why did he keep asking that question, she lamented to herself. She lowered her eyes, longing to tell him how much she loved him, but knowing he would then force her to stay. She turned away, trembling, and hoped that he wouldn't guess her true feelings.

NINE

Selvam waited in silence, then said, "Julia, you didn't answer my question."

Julia whirled around toward him with a burning counterquestion. "Where were you, Selvam? Nirmala was upset. What were you doing?"

Selvam's face hardened and his eyes became remote. "It doesn't relate to you."

Those words stung her more ruthlessly than the pushing and shoving of the women who had excluded her because she didn't belong.

Selvam relented. "I tried to come earlier. Anyway I came in time for *nalangu.*"

Julia saw the concern in his eyes and she softened. "Well, I guess it must have been important."

"Yes, it was very important. But I can't tell you about it now. In any case," he said softly, "it's nothing you should worry about."

Julia thought that the *nalangu* ceremony would be over shortly and people would start to move toward the commissary. "I guess we'd better go back," she said.

"Wait." He grabbed her hand. "I have something for you." He led her into the clinic anteroom, where he unlocked one of the cabinets. The nurse on duty popped her head in and, seeing familiar staff, gave a short greeting, then left.

Julia could never resist surprises, no matter how small or insignificant. She stood anxiously while he pulled out a flat, pink box with a picture of a smiling goddess on the lid.

"You should have a decent sari for Nirmala's marriage," he said as he opened the box and presented her with the neatly folded silk cloth.

Julia's mouth dropped. She stared at the rich violet-blue silk, embroidered throughout with a petite motif of light green leaves and vines. She unfolded it carefully to reveal the heavy woven brocade of gold on the border and end.

"Selvam," she whispered in a high, childlike voice, "it's beautiful." She had seen one like it on a movie star and Mrs. Arokiaswamy had one, though not quite so rich looking. She swallowed. "It must have cost more than Nirmala's wedding sari."

"Perhaps," he said smiling.

She arched her brows, because Nirmala's red silk wedding sari was covered with gold brocade, more gold than this sari, and yet the quality of the silk and the amount of skilled craftsmanship must have made this one more expensive. "I can't accept it," she said with finality, pushing it back toward him.

"If you don't accept it, what can I do? I'll have to burn it." Selvam's eyes twinkled with laughter, as he took out his gold cigarette lighter. Julia clutched the sari to her and stepped back. Selvam laughed out loud and put his lighter away. "Women always like pretty clothes, is it not? A way to a woman's heart."

Julia flashed with anger and was about to throw the sari at him when he stopped her by putting his hand on her cheek. "Now let me give you pretty things. Let me love

142

you at least, even if you don't share the same feelings for me." He smiled at her fondly, and his even black brows looked serene over his leaf-shaped eyes with their inward glint of pain.

Then he backed away with a surge of energy to retrieve an ivory inlaid, rosewood box from the cabinet. The ivory, yellowed with age, formed the design of a cowherd maiden walking barefooted near a tree, with a young calf following behind.

"I want to lend this to you for the wedding," said Selvam as he handed it over to her.

Julia looked perplexed, thinking that he was referring to the box.

"Go on, open it," coaxed Selvam.

Julia obeyed, and inside she saw the most exquisite jewelry set she had ever seen, at least other than at a museum. On a bed of royal blue satin was a gold necklace with fiery blue stones, gleaming through the depth of their blueness even under the forty-watt bulb hanging from above. Matching it was a set of stud earrings with umbrella-shaped attachments called *jimikkis* and a pair of heavy gold bangles with blue stones alternating with small gold filigree leaves. The tiniest pearls of rose and bluish iridescence hung from the *jimikki* attachments and the center pendant of the necklace.

"It's magnificent."

"It was my mother's," said Selvam. "When she died, my father gave all her jewels to me."

"I couldn't wear it," she whispered, as if involved in some clandestine scheme.

"Actually *cinnamma* and Leela spoke about how you should have some jewels to wear for the wedding. I overheard them and suggested lending some of my mother's."

"Did they really talk about that?" Julia smiled. She felt happy to know they had thought about her.

"Yes. It didn't even occur to me. I was so busy. Of course they didn't think it proper for an unmarried girl to wear the sapphire set, but I insisted."

"Sapphires!"

"Certainly," he said in a matter-of-fact tone. "My father is a big doctor and wealthy as well. My mother's side was also wealthy. They gave a very large dowry including one hundred sovereigns of gold and other jewels. I wanted to give some for Nirmala, but *appa* said everything had been fixed for her."

"What about Rita?" asked Julia. "She only has about six sovereigns."

Selvam smiled and pinched Julia's cheek. "You like Rita, don't you?"

Julia nodded. "Who can't help but like her?"

"Well, Miss Julia, you don't have to worry. I'm taking care of everything. Rita will have half of my mother's jewels. Her father and my mother were sister and brother, so actually the jewels came from her family in the first place."

"And what do you plan to do with the rest of them?" asked Julia, thinking he could give them all to Rita, since his wife, some rich lady doctor, would come to him heavily endowed with her own jewelry. She wanted him to give them all to Rita after the way he had been deceiving the poor, innocent girl, but she suddenly flushed when she noticed Selvam raise his eyebrow in surprise. Her question had been quite improper.

"Perhaps, my dear Julia," he said in a voice as soft as velvet, "they will someday be yours, hmm? That's what I have in mind."

Yes, thought Julia, he wouldn't have to give any jewelry

to his wife, but to a keep . . . She remembered with a painful lump in her throat how Selvam had asked, after explaining about keeps, if she had noticed all of Kavitha's jewelry. So Selvam planned to keep her as well as his father had kept Kavitha. That much was clear. But the idea in no way pleased her. Infuriated, she lashed out at him with a saucy voice, "Though flattery may get you everywhere, Selvam, bribery will not."

He cocked his head and pressed his lips together firmly, obviously surprised by her words. Then quickly he drew his lips into a smile, ready for battle. "Good, Julia. You're not to be lured by trinkets. So . . . what if I offer you something even more valuable?"

"What?" asked Julia, suddenly wishing to escape.

"Myself, my love." His black-brown eyes twinkled under the pale light.

Julia lowered her eyes and moaned inwardly. Then Selvam took her into his arms, gently because she was holding the sari and jewelry box. She looked up at him and saw the burning passion on his face. She trembled with anticipation and then his lips claimed hers, softly, sensuously, as his arms enfolded her and his hands kneaded her back. She closed her eyes and almost dropped what she was holding while waves of desire spread through her.

Then he pulled back and said quietly, after a deep breath, "I think they'll be ready for dinner now."

"Yes, of course. They'll be wondering where you are."

Selvam and Julia became clumsy as they started to walk out of the clinic. Then he turned to her and held her shoulders. His eyes darted over her face.

"Julia, in all seriousness now, I must have your answer soon. Come to me on Saturday after Nirmala and my parents have left. It may be the last time for us to be

145

together." He kissed her briefly on the forehead with soft, warm lips.

Julia hesitated at the idea of being alone with him at the house, but then remembered that the servants would be there. A perfect situation, chaperones who couldn't understand English. "All right, I'll come."

But she wondered why it might be the last time for them to be together when her departure flight was scheduled Sunday after next, and she wouldn't have to leave the clinic until a week from the coming Saturday.

During the wedding mass early Friday morning at the old Portuguese church in Tamaraiyur, the groom, a thin, nervous man in his late twenties, solemnly took up the *tali,* the gold marriage amulet shaped like a small Bible. It was strung on a thick, cotton string which had been dyed in turmeric. As the shrill flute and crude leather drums filled the air with wild, palpitating music, he tied it around Nirmala's neck.

Julia sat on a wooden bench on the ladies' side, weighted down by the heavy silk sari and jewelry Selvam had given her. The church had no fans and Julia could feel perspiration tickling her in small rivulets. This was the hottest season of the year, and perhaps the hottest day of the season, she guessed.

Selvam stood near the front row on the men's side, leaning against the ancient wall. He, too, looked uncomfortable and hot in his navy blue suit.

While the groom struggled to tie the *tali* string with the help of some plump aunt, Julia's and Selvam's eyes met, but they didn't smile. She closed her eyes and, as she offered a prayer for Nirmala and her groom, she prayed that Selvam would someday tie the *tali* around her neck. A completely hopeless wish. When she opened her eyes,

146

he was still looking at her. And then the music stopped. The groom had finished tying the *tali.*

Julia saw Selvam briefly in the main hall of Dr. Arokiaswamy's house during the wedding feast. She sat cross-legged on the floor in a row with other guests. Except for the family—Selvam and his *cinnamma*—this would be the last group to eat, Julia imagined. They had wanted to seat her with the first group, but she had gone to check in at the clinic.

Although Julia liked *biriyani,* she had a hard time eating the buttery pilau and vegetables on the plantain leaf in front of her. Selvam was helping to serve the food, and she felt butterflies in her stomach from his solicitous behavior toward her. She hoped no one would notice or suspect anything.

"You aren't eating," he said, standing in front of her with a steel bucket of eggplant chutney in one hand and a ladle in the other. "Would you like a fork? I think *cinnamma* may have one somewhere." He had taken off his jacket, and the sleeves of his white silk shirt were rolled up above his elbows.

"No, thank you. I'm quite used to eating with my hands."

He started to dish some vegetables onto her leaf. She immediately reacted—as she frequently had to do in India —by holding her hand spread out above her food. "No, no, I can't eat anymore."

"You're going to reduce down to a skeleton," he murmured, shaking his head, and then he moved on to the next person.

After Julia finished, she quickly folded the plantain leaf, as was custom, and rose to her feet before Selvam could fill her leaf up again.

She walked out to the back veranda to a large bucket

147

of water at the edge. She was about to take the plastic cup hooked over the side of the bucket, when Selvam appeared beside her.

"Allow me," he said in his deep, quiet voice. He dipped the cup into the water and began pouring it over Julia's extended hand. He towered over her as she rubbed her hand under the trickling water. He stood very near, much nearer than appropriate, she thought, and hoped people wouldn't see them.

"You are such a good host," she remarked nervously.

"I'm just doing what anyone would do for his sister's wedding, just my duty." Then he lowered his voice to a bare whisper. "Except that with you, Julia, I do it with all my affection."

She blushed and quickly wiped her hand on the towel he offered.

He continued, "Don't forget to see me tomorrow, my dear one."

Before anyone could see them together, or hear whatever else he might say, she darted out of the house.

Julia didn't see Selvam again. The groom's maternal uncle and family vacated her house, and most of the guests left the clinic. The wedding party diminished to just the closest circle of relatives for the wedding night.

Julia lay on her wooden cot that night thinking about the next day and her rendezvous with Selvam as she had come to refer to it, about whether or not she should go to him.

But there was no need to spend a sleepless night in contemplating because she knew from the beginning, when Selvam had invited her, that she would go. She knew it even when Leela confronted her under the banyan tree in the late afternoon.

"Where are you going?" Leela knitted her brows, searching Julia's face. Julia knew she had guessed.

"To Dr. Arokiaswamy's house."

"But the doctor and his wife left with the others for Vailangani, to visit the Vailangani *Mata*. They will not return till late tomorrow."

"I know," said Julia. She had been to the Our Lady of Vailangani Basilica and knew they would stay for mass on Sunday. "Selvam invited me for tiffin."

"For tiffin?" She raised her black eyebrows.

"I can manage him." It suddenly occurred to Julia how she could turn the visit to her own advantage. For too long she had felt trapped by the dilemma of whether or not to leave Selvam. Tonight she would throw the dilemma back to him. She would devise some plan in which he would be faced with a painful decision.

"But he is alone. He sent all the servants away."

"He did?" asked Julia. "How do you know?" She felt a tingle of fear travel up her spine.

"Tetru told me he gave them some money and sent them away for all the day . . . and night."

Julia looked toward the imposing pink-beige house a quarter of a mile away. Inside Selvam waited for her. She looked back to Leela, worried.

"Still," she said, trying to calm her pounding heart, "I can manage him, even alone. You yourself said he's a good person."

"He is a man, and no man can be good with too much temptation."

Julia didn't have to be reminded that he was a man, all man in every way. Her face flushed at the thought of him. "I'm not afraid. You're simply making too much out of this. Selvam and I have much more in common than just physical attraction, and we like to be together."

149

"You have so much in common because I wrote to Joseph all about you. I planned it because Joseph was not getting married and I so wanted to have his babies playing around the clinic, to hear their sweet voices."

"But why me?" asked Julia with a crescendo of pain in her voice. "Why not some girl in his caste, a lady doctor or someone like that?"

"I thought you would be perfect for him, since he stayed in America so long time, and because he refused to marry any girl when he came six years ago on leave. I thought you would be just what he wanted."

"He does want me, but not in the way you planned."

"It is all so terrible." Leela sighed deeply.

"It would have happened anyway, without any encouragement. We were already suited, or perhaps destined, for each other—that's what it seems—except that marriage is not to be a part of it. And I *am* going to see him now, whether or not you approve."

Julia started to walk away, milling over possible plans.

"I do not approve, but I will offer my prayers for you."

Julia smiled briefly at Leela's dramatic tone, at the over-concern. Selvam was a passionate man, but he was decent, despite his sometimes rough appearance and his teasing and taunting. She knew, as he had told her earlier, that he would never do anything to a woman against her will. And that very trait would be an important part of her plan, she thought.

When she reached the veranda, however, she had second thoughts. Selvam, dressed in his red and yellow batik *kaili,* sat cross-legged on the large plank swing. His white shirt was unbuttoned, revealing the tangle of black hair on his chest. He looked up at her from a book and stared with the same intensity as when he first stared at her in the hotel lobby, but his face was much more serious now.

"I thought you wouldn't come," he said, then smiled.

"Why? I'm not late, am I?" The sun still sent its after-noon glow to the pink wall. The wedding party, including Selvam's parents, had left only thirty minutes before.

"No, quite on time." His voice held a certain tender-ness. "You look so young now, like a little girl."

Julia wore a pretty violet and yellow print sari she had borrowed from Rita. She had only a light coat of lipstick on and her hair was pulled back by a barrette. But a little girl? Well, if he thought so, then so much the better for her plan.

"I think," he continued, "perhaps I'm rushing you too much. If you were a few years older . . ."

"I'm twenty-three."

"But can you count the two years here in India, tucked away at this clinic? No, Julia, you're quite a bit younger than that lovely apparition I first saw in the Queen's Pal-ace Hotel. You need more time, a lot more time to develop any feelings of love, mature love, and then come to some decision about us."

Julia sat down in a cream-painted rattan chair. She suddenly figured out how she could catch him off-balance and lure him to the point at which his scruples would come into conflict with his desires, to the point at which he would have to make the final decision. It was all so simple. She would agree to be his mistress.

She hoped that even though he had suggested the idea in the first place, he would balk at it if he had to make the final decision. Then he would either propose marriage or send her away. And if he accepted her offer to be his keep, she could always back down.

"Selvam," she said lightly, as if testing his reaction, "I don't want to leave India. I think I want to stay here

151

. . . with you. But only if you really want it that way." Her face reddened.

"You think?" He bowed his head a little and smiled. The gleam in his eyes danced through his long, dark lashes. "Come on, let's have some tiffin. Only when your commitment is as strongly grounded as the roots of a mango tree would you be ready for me, my dear. I don't want any later regrets."

He hadn't accepted and he hadn't balked at the idea either. Instead he had thrown the decision back to her. And she certainly would not and could not brazenly accept his offer. She waited to develop some other tactic.

Selvam went into the house and returned with a bottle of scotch, two glasses, and a bowl of ice. "It's not exactly as romantic as wine."

"Selvam!" she gasped. "It's illegal. Tamil Nadu's a dry state."

"No, dear. This is from the plane. They allow two half bottles." He put ice in the glasses and began to pour.

"But I don't drink . . . a little wine now and then, but not that kind of liquor."

"I intend to make this a poetry party," he said seeming to ignore her, smiling with his teasing eyes. "I'll start with those immortal words of Ogden Nash, 'Candy is dandy but liquor is quicker.' "

"Not a very good start," said Julia in mock prudishness, but she took the glass he offered. "Not at all conducive to making me want to drink this."

Secretly she contemplated how the liquor would actually help out in her plan and took a long drink, choking as she did. If he had been too astute in avoiding the decision in a rational situation, then she would force him to make the decision in an emotional situation. In effect, she would allow him to seduce her. The decision would be his, but she could always stop him. Hopefully, though, he would take the moral choice—marriage or breaking off from her.

Selvam smiled at her mischievously. "Then let's start with Omar Khayyam." He picked up his book and held it almost reverently.

> "A Book of Verses underneath the Bough,
> A Jug of Wine, a Loaf of Bread—and Thou
>   Beside me singing in the Wilderness—
> Oh, Wilderness were Paradise enow!"

"Beautiful," whispered Julia. She took another long sip from her glass.

"Shall I continue?"

"Yes, please." She felt the first surge of intoxication descending through her body, and poetry seemed so right at this time, like another very sweet intoxicant.

Selvam turned directly to the poems which he obviously had planned to read. After several poems, he read Robert Herrick's "To the Virgins to Make Much of Time," and then Andrew Marvell's "To His Coy Mistress."

"Enough, enough," said Julia after listening to the deep resonance of his voice, seductive in itself without poetry. She could feel the liquor saturating her body. Time slowed down and her movements became disconnected from her mind. Despite that, the message in the last poems was clear. He was trying to coax her to come to a decision, a definite decision. The time had come, she thought, to start implementing her plan.

"You are right, Julia. Very unfair of me to use poetry. Did you ever finish *Shilappadikaram*?"

She immediately glared at him. *Shilappadikaram*, the book he had given her, that had first exposed her to the world of courtesans and keeps. "No," she said.

He looked surprised. Then he put the book down and poured her more scotch. "I wish you'd read it, Julia."

He had barely touched his drink, so his voice remained quite steady. By contrast Julia's face had reddened and she had to put forth much effort to coordinate her movements. It was a new experience for her, and although she had always disliked drunkenness in others, she could now understand why people drank. A pleasant, glowing feeling soothed the anguish she had been feeling—it seemed for eternity—from being torn between her love for Selvam and the need to leave him.

"One last poem by Omar Khayyam," said Selvam as he finished pouring the scotch.

Julia knew he was plying her with liquor. She also knew that he wasn't drinking. But she continued to drink, smiling and thinking that her plan was moving along very well. She drank the fiery liquid as if it were prescribed medicine.

Selvam took up the book.

"Ah, my Beloved, fill the Cup the clears
To-day of past Regret and future Fears:
    To-morrow!—Why, To-morrow I may be
Myself with Yesterday's Sev'n thousand Years."

"How beautifully appropriate, Selvam. I love . . ." She almost told him what he had longed to hear, what the emotional side of her had longed to tell him, but her mind caught up with her tongue. "I love the way you read poetry. Your voice, it has so much expression, not maudlin or overdramatic, but so deep, so . . ."

"I wish you'd love me as you do my voice, Julia." He put his book down and stood up. The *kaili,* reaching to his ankles, accented the narrowness of his hips and the broad-

154

ness of his chest. "Come now, I want to ask you for your help."

She stood up and, as part of her plan, pretended to lose her balance. But did she pretend? The liquor had affected her more than she had imagined.

Selvam caught her in his arms. "I guess you're not used to drinking."

"What help do you want from me?" she asked innocently, looking up into his intent face, marveling as always at his black hair falling across his forehead. She was glad she had become drunk. It excused what she was about to do, what she had wanted to do from the start. She reached up and raked her fingers through his thick hair.

Selvam laughed, then swallowed. His arm jostled around her waist to steady her wavering stance. "I see you love my hair too."

"Yes," she whispered. She touched his lips with her finger. "And your lips . . . and your eyes."

He closed his eyes. His thick lashes skirted his cheeks and he sighed slowly. When he opened his eyes, they pierced through her with fire. His arm tightened around her and his other hand clutched her chin and face, hurting her with his pressure. His lips descended to hers with force, and she slid her arms up around his neck. Between kisses and crushing embraces, he maneuvered her into the house, bolted the door behind them, and then took her to the yellow-walled guest room.

He walked her to the old wooden bed with a thin cotton mattress.

"Selvam . . ." She started to speak, but it sounded more like a protest than the beginning of a love confession, and she didn't want it to sound like a protest.

"No, Julia," he interrupted. He pushed her gently

down. "No more coyness. I know what you want, and what I want, and there's no stopping now."

He pulled the loose end of her sari away, revealing her thin sari blouse. His lips traveled down her throat and onto her neck and along the low, scooped neckline of her blouse.

Passion welled up in her chest and she decided she could afford to abandon her self-control temporarily, because she knew she could stop him at any time with the slightest motion of protest. Her arms pulled him toward her, and his whole body pressed against hers. His lips found hers, opening them with their force. She could hardly breathe from his weight, but then he shifted to the side and started to stroke her face.

"Julia, my Julia. I don't want to hurt you. I promise I won't."

"I know, Selvam. I trust you not to hurt me." Her words were slurred, but she knew exactly what was happening. She would have to control herself from succumbing to the dizziness of her own desires, desires she had never known before. It was all new to her, the effect of the liquor, the much more intense effect of Selvam's kisses and lovemaking. But she knew she had control. Her plan had taken shape. She laughed lightly inside herself because for once Selvam was under her power.

Selvam rested on his elbow. His hand propped up his head, and he looked down at her lovingly, almost thankful for her compliance, almost not believing what was happening.

Julia grew impatient. She reached for his free hand and brought it to her lips and her cheek. She looked at him with inviting eyes, but instead of immediately moving, he started to speak.

"Julia, I don't want you to think that I intended this before. I mean inviting you here, giving you scotch."

"Reading me poetry," she added with a smile and a sweet bravado in her voice. He felt guilty, she thought.

"I swear, Julia, I didn't intend ... ." His eyes closed and he started to reach for her.

"I know," she said weakly.

Their lips met. This time he nibbled gently at them, then at her cheek, only lightly pressing his body against hers. She felt him deftly reach for the hooks on the front of her blouse, and with a smoothness and speed that astonished her, he had her blouse unfastened. Then without interrupting his kiss, he unhooked her bra. She lay back, taking her lips from his, and gasped in a light, heart-stopping manner.

"Julia." An echo of desperation resounded from his deep, husky voice. "I don't want you to regret . . . I could stop."

His breathing became heavy and she could see the struggle on his face and in the flexing of his muscles. He had reached that moment of painful decision as she had predicted so well, and she was not going to help him one way or the other. The fact that she was drunk made her plan all the better. Would he dare take advantage of a drunken woman who was slightly out of her mind?

"Could you stop now?" Her voice trembled, but she gave him an alluring smile.

"No," he gulped and descended on her with such strength, kissing and grabbing her to him, that she suddenly felt fearful and started to struggle.

He was supposed to stop, and then come to a realization that his idea of making her his keep was unacceptable to him. He was supposed to propose marriage, or at least give her up. She had no recourse now but to fight, and hope

157

that what he had said was true, that he wouldn't do anything to a girl against her will.

Her movements of protest, however, must have seemed like movements of passion, because he was only spurred on. Without her knowing how it happened, he had pushed aside her blouse and bra, and his hard chest was rubbing against her tender breasts. And then her fear gave way to expectation. Her whole body pulsated and her struggle turned to deep, heaving breaths as her body pressed against his.

She realized that she had completely lost control and Selvam would guide her expertly, without any pain as he had promised, to the culmination of that joy shared by man and woman. Her plan had failed, and she moaned softly with ecstasy as his hand began to travel up her thigh, lifting and crumpling her sari.

TEN

Julia didn't hear the voice at first, but when Selvam pulled away suddenly, leaving her in a fever of desire, she heard Siva shouting.

"Doctor, Saar . . . Dr. Selvanathan."

Selvam was standing up, retucking his *kaili* at the waist. It had apparently become loose while he was on the bed with her. Julia weakly tried to bring her blouse over her bare breasts, but it had become caught behind her, and she felt too weak to struggle with it.

Selvam went to the window and threw open the top shutter. He called back to Siva, "*Enna appa? Enna atthu?*"

Julia reached for the bedsheet and pulled it over her, while Selvam and Siva spoke to each other in Tamil. She understood that there was an emergency at the clinic. By the description it sounded like a little girl with appendicitis.

Selvam pulled out some clothes from the almirah. Julia turned her head away from him as he quickly dressed.

"So shy now, huh?" said Selvam from across the room.

Julia kept her head turned away from him, and started crying softly. Even though they had been interrupted before anything could happen, she couldn't deny that she had wanted him. She had not protested in the end as she

159

had planned, and now his words sounded so crude. Damn her plans, she thought, and cried harder.

"Why, Julia?" His voice became very gentle, fringed with concern. He walked over to her as he fastened his belt.

"Go on," she said, looking up at him. "Go to your emergency."

"Please stay here, Julia. I can't let you go like this. And I'm not sure where the house keys are. Bolt the doors and wait for me."

Julia nodded. She just wanted him to leave quickly, to help the little girl, and to free her of his overpowering presence. "I'll stay," she whispered.

Selvam bent down and brushed her tears with his thumb. Then he kissed her on the forehead. Julia didn't look up at him, but she felt the warmth of his breath.

"If I come late," he said, "there's some food in the kitchen. Go ahead and eat. I'll eat later."

Julia waited until she heard the front door open and close, then she stood up and dressed herself. She watched him out the window. He walked quickly away from the house toward the clinic with a confident stride.

Even with him gone, she felt his presence in the house, still felt his power as she walked out of his room. Previously she had thought of the house as Dr. Arokiaswamy's, but now it clearly belonged to Selvam. Perhaps it always had, and that was what gave it the imposing powerfulness she always felt when she visited.

The sun had set and the rooms were rapidly becoming dark, so she bolted the doors and turned on a few lights. The heat of the day hadn't subsided much. Julia, hot and damp with perspiration, headed toward the bathroom, barely reaching it before she became sick from all the scotch. She felt relieved to rid herself of the liquor, and vowed never to drink like that again.

Hours later, after a bath and a nap, the drugging effects of the scotch diminished. She felt weak, but refreshed. When Selvam returned, she went to unbolt the door, neatly dressed in her sari, with her hair combed and clasped in the barrette.

"How did it go?" she asked. "Appendectomy?"

"Yes. The girl's fine now. She had come by bullock cart. The condition was acute, but we had no serious complications."

"Who assisted?"

"Leela, Rita, Ravi, and Perumal. When the other doctor comes, our work will be so much easier," he said, looking about absently. His posture seemed a bit wilted from the exertion he had just been through, and from the heat.

Julia asked with pretended nonchalance, "A lady doctor?"

"Yes, that'd be ideal."

Ideal, she thought. *Ideal for the clinic and ideal for him!* Her throat became constricted with jealousy for this unknown lady doctor.

"I think I'd better go now," she said with difficulty.

"Julia, my Julia." His voice flowed with tenderness. "I can see you're still upset. You're trembling." He clasped her two cheeks in his hands and looked down at her with soft, questioning eyes. "You didn't eat, did you?"

"No," she stated flatly, turning her gaze away from him.

"Then let's eat." He took her chin with his hand and shook it a little, smiling a friendly smile, as remote from the passion he had shown earlier, as any of his expressions could be. "You needn't be afraid of me." He released her

161

and stepped back. "Now, could you heat up some food for us? I want to take a bath first. It's so hot today."

Julia smiled and blushed as she busied herself in the kitchen, thinking how it all seemed like they were playing a grown-up version of house. When they went into the dining room to eat, Selvam sat at the head of the table where Dr. Arokiaswamy usually sat. He wore a fresh blue-and-white striped *kaili* and a white shirt. Julia stood by him and served.

"Eat with me, Julia," he said. "I don't go along with that custom of the wife eating only after the husband is finished. I'd want my wife to eat with me."

Julia's heart jumped. He had spoken as if he planned to marry her, but perhaps he, too, was caught up in the spirit of playing house.

"And what else would you expect of your wife?" She sat down at the side of the table near him and started serving herself some rice, *sambar,* vegetables, and half the ome-lette she had prepared.

"Well, one thing, I'd expect her to read the books I gave her." He smiled, but his tone had an edge of seriousness. He kneaded the rice and *sambar* with his hand and began eating.

Julia's heart jumped again. She wondered if he had some idea of marrying her, but she didn't wish to pursue the matter of his expectations. He might go on to add how much dowry and gold jewelry he expected, and that he hoped to marry a lady doctor.

After the meal, Julia prepared to leave, but Selvam protested. "Don't go yet. I told you earlier I wanted your help . . . and then we became sidetracked some way." His devilish smile made him look the handsome rogue he so often appeared to her.

Julia felt the exasperation of her reply before she gave

it much thought. "How can I help you, Selvam? You're the last person in the world who needs help from anyone."

"That's not true. Everyone needs help and advice at times. Now, after my father retires and goes to Madras, I'm planning to make some changes in this house. I've already thought about painting the outside a light blue color. What do you think?"

"Yes. That'd be very nice."

"But I don't quite know what to do with the interior. It looks so cluttered here, especially with all those pictures on the walls. *Appa* will be taking some with him, but which ones should I take down? I'd like to make it as simple as possible."

Julia thought for a moment. "I don't know. It's a problem. They could be arranged more artistically, but which saint would you discard? Which family or clinic photograph? Each one of them has some special significance. Could you take down the one of the guardian angel protecting the little boy and girl? I don't think so." The problem perplexed her. A few Indian houses were simple and elegant in the Western way, but most were cluttered with pictures of deities and family members. And once a picture had been hung up, how could it be taken down?

Selvam smiled broadly. "I see your point. But then, do you mind it this way?"

"No, I think it's very beautiful in its own way. I think perhaps it expresses a desire to be surrounded by more and more people, if not possible in real life, at least in pictures." Then Julia thought about how her aunt and uncle had not wanted her and how it contrasted with the desires of Leela and Raman and everyone at the clinic to keep her with them, how Selvam also wanted her, even if only as a keep. And how right now he seemed to be stalling just to keep her with him.

"I'm glad you like the pictures," he said.

It suddenly occurred to Julia why he was asking her advice. He wanted to prepare the house for his wife. That's why he needed a woman's advice. "So then, do you think your wife might like them?"

"Oh, I know she will," said Selvam, missing the pain on Julia's face. "Now I want to know which room you think would be the best for a bedroom. There are two downstairs and three upstairs."

Selvam took her hand and led her through the house. She had never been upstairs before and was delighted by the grandeur of the immense house. They ended the tour in the largest upstairs bedroom. Jasmine chains still covered the bedposts and canopy of the large, wooden cot, obviously used for Nirmala's wedding night. The cotton mattress and woven bedsheets were still strewn with jasmine and rose petals.

"This is a perfect room," said Julia right away. "See, you have windows on three sides. You'll be able to get the southern breeze. An attached bath and dressing room. This seems larger than the main hall."

"It is. Come here." He led her through a door that went directly onto the terrace. When he flicked on the lights, it turned into a garden of potted plants and trellised creepers.

"Some rattan furniture would be just perfect here." Julia's voice trembled with the thought that she would never share this garden terrace with Selvam.

Selvam leaned down and kissed her lightly, brushing his lips against hers. Then he led her back into the room. "I plan to make this completely American style," he said, "with an air conditioner, curtains, wall-to-wall carpeting, built-in closets instead of almirahs, and a king-size bed with mattress and box springs."

164

She raised her eyebrows. "So you had already decided on this room."

"Yes, but I wanted to get your reaction."

Before bringing your wife here, she added silently to herself, but said to him, "How would you get all those things? I mean, can you get them in India?"

"Sure. Everything's available here for a price," he said, looking away.

"So then you can keep your wife in comfort." Her voice was constricted with pain.

Selvam turned to her and held her gaze with his piercing eyes. Then he pulled her to him. Julia clung to him, yielding to his pressure as he kissed her forehead and lips.

But then she pushed him away. All this, the house, the bedroom, the mattress and box-spring bed . . . and his kisses, all were for his wife. She couldn't bear the thought.

"Okay, Julia, I won't touch you." He backed away from her. "I won't ruin your virtue. Perhaps you'll never trust me again."

He had misunderstood her, but she didn't stop to explain. She rushed down the stairs. "It's very late. I must go," she called back.

Selvam went down the stairs behind her. "Wait. I must tell you something."

Julia stopped by the front door to hear what he had to say.

"I'm going away tomorrow after mass."

She turned and looked up at him. As if out of breath she asked, "Will you be back in time . . . before I leave?"

"I should be back late Monday night. But are you really leaving next Saturday? You said this afternoon . . ."

"And as you said, I haven't come to any definite decision. It seems now I will leave." She gave him a sharp look. "So where are you going tomorrow? What are you planning to do?"

"I can't tell you now. Only that it's important and you'll learn about it soon."

Julia opened the door. She felt she had to escape before she ended up staying. She hardly heard him.

"Just one last kiss, Julia. I think there won't be another chance for us to be together. It'll get very rough around here when I return." He hesitated, then his voice filled with pain. "Oh, my dearest one, make your decision to stay. If only you could love me." He pulled her into a tight embrace and kissed her harshly while she wilted in his arms. His lips burned hers like a hot, searing brand. She felt the hardness of his body, the body of a rugged sailor returning after many months at sea. But he wasn't returning to her, they were parting.

He pushed her away from him, still holding her shoulders. He looked down with gleaming eyes and told her, "Go now, *ma,* but don't leave India."

She turned and left. Her legs moved heavily, as if she were wading through a wet paddy field. Her whole mind and body felt completely devastated. And she wondered where he was going after mass. Why the mystery?

Early the next morning Julia waited for Rita and Susheela while they dressed. She sat on a bed in the nurses' residence and watched them wind their chiffon saris around themselves as skillfully as any young, fashion-conscious Indian girls. Julia always felt refreshed to be in their presence. Lata was taking a bath, getting ready for her shift.

"Where were you yesterday?" asked Rita. "We had an emergency. I sent Siva to fetch you, but he said you were not at home."

Julia felt relieved that Leela and Selvam hadn't said anything, so that not only was her virtue safe, as Selvam had put it, but also her reputation. She felt glad Rita and the others wouldn't have a bad impression of her, especially just before she was about to leave India. She smiled. "Oh, I went for a walk. Siva must have come after I left."

The girls didn't press the matter. They were busy rubbing talc on their faces and making small, black dots on their foreheads.

"Julia," said Rita. "I want to show you what Joe *athan* gave me." She unlocked her almirah and pulled out an assortment of boxes: three flat jewelry boxes, some small earring boxes, and a round bangle box.

Julia looked with astonishment as Rita opened each one to reveal all the jewelry, a set of pearl necklace, earrings, and bangles; a red stone set; a plain gold set; chains and gold bangles in all different styles; loop earrings with swans set on the inner part of the loops and tiny gold beads beneath.

"Fifty sovereigns," said Susheela, looking at them with her large, black eyes.

"And these are real rubies," said Rita without any intention of bragging.

"Which are more valuable, Julia," asked Susheela, "rubies or emeralds?"

Julia knew they were weighing Rita's jewels against Nirmala's. "It depends, I think, on the quality of the stones. I'm no jeweler. Nirmala's emeralds are not as bright and shiny as these."

She had seen Nirmala parading her emeralds in front of the girls and she now saw the satisfied expressions on their faces. "But we must go to mass now," she added. "Dr. Selvanathan will be waiting for us, and we shouldn't be thinking about jewelry."

167

In front of the clinic commissary Selvam stood leaning against the jeep. He wore tan pants and an ink blue shirt.

"Three lovely maidens. What a treat for me," he said.

Rita and Susheela giggled, but Julia remained silent.

After mass Selvam let the girls out of the jeep at the clinic. Because of all that had passed between them the night before, Julia kept her head lowered and didn't look at him as she went into her house.

A few minutes later, however, she looked out her window, surprised to see the jeep still parked outside on the road between her house and the clinic commissary. Then she saw Selvam emerge from the dormitory carrying two suitcases. Rita followed close behind him, throwing her head back. Her whole face beamed with a smile. Julia thought she looked as radiant as a new bride, and then she gasped with horror at the last thought. Selvam threw the luggage in the back and escorted Rita to the door where he held it for her to get in.

Soon they were off down the road and Julia stood at the window stunned, her face a chalky white. Selvam and Rita were eloping, but why? Everyone wanted them to get married—Dr. Arokiaswamy, Rita's mother. Why, then? It didn't make sense.

Julia's mind spun and she felt a very strong headache taking over. No, it couldn't be marriage, she thought. They wouldn't have had to elope. Then what? The idea came suddenly. The pieces fell together. Selvam was a passionate man, a man with needs that had to be met. Since she had not complied, then apparently Rita would. So, Selvam really did intend to emulate his father. And if Rita wasn't good enough for marriage, she was good enough for . . .

But sweet, innocent Rita? Selvam might be using the jewels to tempt her. Julia shuddered at the thought, but she knew it had to be true: Selvam was making Rita his keep!

The rest of the day seemed like a nightmare. Dr. and Mrs. Arokiaswamy returned in the afternoon from their pilgrimage to Vailangani. Dr. Arokiaswamy noticed his son's absence and soon found out about Rita's absence, and that they had left together. Everyone at the clinic was questioned, but no one, not even Susheela or Lata, knew why they had left or where they were going.

On Monday the whole clinic staff fell into a state of shock and hushed gossip. And when Selvam returned without Rita in the middle of the night, Julia knew she probably wouldn't be able to see him alone again, just as he had predicted. It didn't take long for the news to trickle down to her. She prepared herself for the worst when Leela stopped by her house Tuesday morning.

"Julia, we must think of some scheme to get Joseph away from the clinic. Dr. Arokiaswamy is very upset. It seems they have been arguing all night."

"Leela, what is it? What did Selvam do with Rita?" She felt an uncontrollable quiver throughout her body. How could she ever have loved such a despicable man? And yet she still loved him and cried inside for Rita.

"It is a terrible blow to the doctor, to his whole family. Joseph took Rita and had her married off to a man from a much lower caste. It is such a stain on the family. It happens sometimes, but it has never happened in Dr. Arokiaswamy's family."

Julia shook her head in surprise, too stunned at first to speak. Then she managed to ask, "But why did he do it?"

"I did not hear the reason," said Leela. "But you please wait. I will send Joseph. You take him somewhere while he and his father can become cooled down."

After Leela left, Julia changed from her nurse's uniform

into a pink T-shirt and maroon wraparound skirt. Half an hour later Selvam came through the door, his tall frame slightly stooped from weariness.

"What is it? Leela said you wanted me to go with you somewhere." His long black lashes so covered his eyes that she could only see a glimmer of the tiredness in his eyes.

"Would you come with me?" she asked tenderly. "I just want to get away for a while."

"I might as well. I came back at two in the morning after so many hours of driving. I won't be very much help at the clinic today." He looked at her affectionately. "Perhaps you should drive."

Julia didn't know where to go. Finally she found herself driving to the tourist lodge.

"So, this is where you want me to come with you," he said, coming out of his sleep.

"It's not what you think, Selvam."

"Oh, then what do you have in mind?" Selvam was wide awake now, trapping Julia in his intense smile. "Wait here."

He left the car and returned in a few minutes. "Come on." He opened the door, and grasping her by the wrist, pulled her out.

"Selvam!"

"Do you want to create a scene? I assure you I wouldn't be embarrassed in the least."

"Oh, you!" she whispered harshly.

He took her into the room and turned on the air-conditioning unit. The artificial breeze made the dark green curtains and bedspread flutter a bit. Julia looked skeptically at the large double bed—a mattress on box springs. She hadn't stayed in such a luxurious hotel since she had come to India.

Selvam pulled the draperies closed, then sat on the bed and removed his shoes.

"What do you plan to do?" she asked, her eyes growing wide.

"I plan to sleep. After I returned, *appa* and I stayed up the rest of the night talking. Come and lie beside me, Julia." He lay down on the soft bed and in the rocking lull of the waves crashing on the shore and the drone of the air conditioner he soon fell asleep.

Julia looked fondly at his relaxed body. In his untroubled face, she saw the good little boy about whom Leela had so often spoken. She lay down beside him, and though she hadn't planned to sleep, she soon fell fast asleep herself.

Before regaining full consciousness, she became aware of a coolness on her feet, arms, and face, which contrasted with a warmth across her waist. Then she awakened with a start. The air conditioner had cooled the room and Selvam, lying on his side, had his arm around her waist. He seemed asleep, but when she looked at his face, his eyes were half open and he was smiling at her. Shallow dimples creased his cheeks. He had never looked so handsome to her and she felt a compelling urge to embrace him and kiss those lips that were both firm and softly sensuous at the same time. However, when his arm started pressing her in toward him, she pulled away and jumped out of the bed.

From across the room she asked, "Is it true? Did you marry Rita off to a lower caste man?"

Selvam propped himself up on his elbow. "Word travels fast."

"It's a small clinic. There aren't any secrets." If she were to become his keep, that, too, wouldn't remain a secret, she thought.

"I didn't marry her off," Selvam protested. "They were

171

childhood sweethearts, but they knew their families wouldn't agree to the marriage."

Astonishment filled her face. "I never guessed."

"That's one reason Rita's mother sent her to the clinic, to keep her away from him. But it didn't work, they wanted to get married. And for a church marriage with banns and all, they needed the help of some relative, so they wrote to me in America."

"All this time you knew. That's why you . . ." She was about to say refused to marry Rita, but instead asked, "Why didn't you tell me?" She stood beside the green curtain, trembling.

"I promised Rita I wouldn't tell anyone. Of course I would've trusted you."

"Then why didn't you help her get married as soon as you returned from America?" It would've spared so much torment, she thought, if she had only known.

"It was a touchy situation. I didn't want to risk any scandal in the family before Nirmala was safely married. Who knows, maybe Rita's mother or father's brothers would retaliate and in some way cause trouble at Nirmala's marriage, maybe even stop it."

"So you waited until after her marriage." All the charges she had been mentally bringing against Selvam rapidly fell away. Her villain was becoming something of a hero.

"Yes, that's right."

"And all those trips you took. The one right before Nirmala's wedding . . ."

"To complete the arrangements for Rita."

"And"—Julia swallowed hard—"that's why you refused to marry Rita."

"Yes. I had to be the one to stop the arrangements for Rita and me. They would've suspected if it had been Rita.

After all"—he smiled wickedly—"I am quite a catch for marriage, is it not? People would immediately be suspicious if any girl refused to marry me." He laughed and lay back on the bed. "Is it not?"

"Selvam, you are very arrogant and very naughty," scolded Julia in a pretended maternal tone.

"Come here. Come to your naughty boy." He held out his arms and Julia went to him.

Selvam's kisses were affectionate, holding no threat of the overwhelming passion he had shown her three days earlier. His arms held her loosely and between kisses his eyes danced merrily over her face and body. Then he leaned back on the bed with his hands behind his head.

Julia's mind raced on with more thoughts. When Selvam had refused to marry Rita, how valid were the reasons he had given? Did he really intend to marry a lady doctor? Perhaps he had just given that as a false reason to stop the arrangements for him and Rita. No, so much more had happened to indicate that he really did want to marry a lady doctor. She didn't feel strong enough now to ask him, but she planned certainly to do so later on, certainly before she left India. And then maybe she wouldn't have to leave. . . .

Another thought made her speak. "What about your father? Is he upset with you about Rita?"

"As I told you before I left, it would cause a lot of trouble. Of course *appa* was upset, very upset. But by the time I talked with him and showed him the letters from Rita and John, he wasn't too upset."

Selvam propped himself up on his elbow and, looking down at Julia, ran his finger lightly over her arm. "Heart of hearts, I don't think he is against intercaste marriages or love marriages, at least not in theory. All of us Christian Indians would accept them in theory," he said laughing, "as long as it doesn't involve us or our own families. *Appa*'s main worry now is the reaction of Rita's mother and that of her father's brothers. Rita had been entrusted to our care, and now all the blame will fall on *appa* and me."

Selvam lay back on the bed again. "Let's not think of family matters, hmm?" He pulled Julia down on top of him and held her head firmly while he kissed her. She felt the length of her body pressed on top of his and blood throbbed warmly through her veins. They slowly rolled until he was pressing down on top of her. She sighed as he stroked her burning cheek.

Julia was thrust out of reality into another world, a world of slow motion in which she was strangely relaxed and strangely tense at the same time, aware of her own feelings as never before, and yet aware of the male aura surrounding and engulfing her—not a fuzzy unidentified male, but Selvam, vivid and sharp, pressing her down into the soft bed with his solid weight. His hand cupped her breast and she moaned. Her nerves tingled with ecstasy.

Then he pulled away abruptly. "Julia," he scolded, "why are you not stopping me?" He shook his head. "We should leave now." He stood up, and Julia's face twitched with guilt. "My dearest Julia, you must come to a definite decision. Then come to me and tell me whether you love me and want to stay. I don't want it this way." He sat on the bed and put on his shoes.

Julia sighed deeply, pulling herself out of the trance. She felt utterly frustrated. "My tickets are for Sunday. I'll have to leave the clinic by Saturday." She hoped to turn the tables and force Selvam to a decision.

"Can't you get some extension? You could write that you're sick and need a few weeks to recover." He looked away from her. "Yes, as your doctor I could write a letter.

We'll have to think up some disease." He returned his gaze to her. "It could be done, Julia."

"I suppose it happens sometimes." Julia's heart sank at the thought of more weeks caught in this anguishing dilemma. She had so hoped he might propose marriage at the last minute.

"I think that's what you need, my dear one, more time, maybe a month or so to decide. Really, I don't want to rush this. You look very mature, like a full-fledged woman. *Ah-gha,* you are a full-fledged woman, but I know you're very young and inexperienced." He stood up from the bed. "Come, we'll go back to the clinic now."

ELEVEN

Julia worked that afternoon at the clinic, despite protests from Leela and Dr. Arokiaswamy that she should take leave for the rest of her stay. She had to keep busy. Her mind whirled with ideas and doubts about what Selvam's intentions were. And she wanted to speak to Leela, but she didn't get that chance until after work, when she invited her for tiffin.

As they drank the sweet, milky coffee, Julia told Leela all that Selvam had told her. She ended with how it had been necessary for him to refuse to marry Rita.

"Julia!" Leela's face lit up like an oil lamp. "See, I told you. Joseph is right for you. And he does want to marry you. He only said he wanted to marry a lady doctor to halt arrangements for him and Rita."

"I don't know, Leela. I just doubt it so much. He's never mentioned marriage to me. Surely he would have by now, if it's his intention."

"But then you also did not ask him about marriage."

"How could I? The man is supposed to ask. And I don't want to marry anyone unless he really, really wants to marry me. Perhaps it's just pride on my part."

"I think it is understandable now. A cultural misunderstanding." Julia could see Leela's eyes gleam. "In India it is the bride's family that must go down. They have to

177

pursue the boy's family. I cannot imagine a boy asking a girl for marriage. The boy and his family would never go down."

"But Selvam lived in America for fifteen years. He knows the customs there. I just can't believe he'd feel that way."

"He is an Indian," protested Leela, "and he has much pride. He always has. He wouldn't go down for anyone, to ask marriage and risk refusal from a girl."

Julia didn't accept Leela's explanation, not at all—Selvam had practically gone to his knees asking her to stay—but she was desperate enough to try anything. If he simply wanted her to ask, if that was all it was, then she certainly could ask.

"Then what should I do? It just seems improper for me to propose marriage to Selvam."

"You must ask. What harm would it do? If he refuses, then that way you would know for sure. But he won't refuse. I know that." Leela nodded her head with certainty. "And when you marry him, I could take the part of your mother for the ceremonies."

Julia smiled weakly. "I'd like that. But I just have so many doubts. It'd be quite humiliating if I ask and he refuses." Leela started to protest, but Julia added, "Oh, I wouldn't mind that. I'd go through anything for Selvam, to be with him, to marry him. That's not the problem."

"Then what is it?" Leela looked disturbed.

"Suppose I ask him to marry me, and suppose he agrees."

"But that is what you want, is it not?"

"No, it's not what I want. It'd be entirely different if he were to propose, but if I propose, and he has no intention of marrying me, he just might agree because he doesn't want to hurt me. I wouldn't want to marry him, not in that way."

"Still it is not a problem, Julia. When you ask, by his reaction you can tell. There is yes and there is yes. You could easily tell the difference. Now it is important you go and ask him this evening. Time is very less for you."

Julia didn't tell her about Selvam's idea for her to stay a few extra weeks. She knew that she must do as Leela advised. Staying longer would only prolong what she had to do.

"But how can I just go and talk to Selvam? His parents are there."

"Then you must go just after dark on a social visit. Dr. Arokiaswamy will then insist Joseph to accompany you home."

Julia's face beamed. "You are very good with plans." Then a worried cloud fell across her eyes. "How could I just go there? If Nirmala were there, I could go to visit her."

"You could return the jewels, is it not?"

Julia had completely forgotten about the sapphire set after she had given it to Leela to lock in her steel almirah. She blushed at her absentmindedness in forgetting to return such valuable jewelry.

"Yes, and I really must return them soon, whether or not I get the courage to ask Selvam to marry me." Julia smiled at her last words.

An hour later, Julia still smiled as she walked in the darkness toward the doctor's house, the jewelry box gripped firmly in her hand. She had taken special care to fix her hair in a neat bun. Leela had made a flower chain for her from jasmines in their common garden, and then had opened up her two almirahs and let Julia select a sari

179

from her vast collection. Julia had chosen one of sky blue chiffon—Selvam's favorite color.

Asking the big question would not be too difficult, she thought. Hearing the answer would be the hard part. A yes would be an answer to her dreams. A no would confirm what she had always suspected, but it would be tolerable. In fact it would relieve her of the burdensome dilemma. She would leave and never see him again. Leela would be there to give her the strength to leave.

The answer she feared the most was a reluctant yes. If he wanted her enough to have her as a keep, he might agree to marriage, especially if he thought he would lose her without marriage. Then the rest of his life he would blame her. She put all those thoughts out of her mind as she approached the house.

The moon had not yet risen, so the road was completely dark. Only a faint amber glow came from the main hall. Even before she reached the veranda she could hear the voices of Dr. Arokiaswamy and Selvam. They spoke rapidly in Tamil. Julia would never think of eavesdropping, but the topic of their conversation made her freeze on the spot.

"Chelledurai has been my close friend for many years," said Dr. Arokiaswamy. "He is also of our caste and he has a daughter with a master's degree in zoology. I have contacted him and informed that we will visit tomorrow evening to see the girl. I would be happy for you to marry my dear friend's daughter. It is a very good family, and prosperous. He is in the cement business."

"I told you"—Selvam's deep voice sent flutters through Julia, but what he said next sent her into a deep shock—"before anything else I want to see the lady doctor. What's her name?"

180

"Rani Rattanaswamy," volunteered Mrs. Arokiaswamy.

"Yes," said Selvam. "First we'll see her tomorrow."

Julia held her breath, then turned and ran back to her house. In her bedroom she started laughing out loud. It suddenly seemed so funny, worrying and worrying about asking Selvam the big question, getting advice and encouragement from Leela, thinking up some pretext to visit his family, and then at last not even having to ask it. She had received his answer loud and clear.

Her laughter turned to tears. "Oh, Selvam!" she cried. She loved him so much. Now her life stretched out before her, a vast desert. She'd never see him again. It would hurt too much. She'd have to leave immediately, tonight.

Julia's eyes were blurred by tears as she packed her belongings. She didn't have much. Everything fit into the two small suitcases and tote bag she had brought to India. For a moment she ran her fingers over the deep violet-blue, embroidered sari Selvam had given her, by far the most valuable and precious of her saris. But then, what would she need it for in America? Perhaps once in a while, just as a conversation piece, she could wear it to a party. Would she ever be able to go to a party again and laugh at jokes, talk gaily to men? She decided to give the sari to Leela. She put it with the sapphire jewelry she planned to leave with Leela to return to Selvam.

By eight o'clock she had packed. Dressed in a two-piece cotton suit of gray-and-red plaid, she went next door. Leela saw her red face and swollen eyes, and immediately rushed to her.

"He refused, is it?" she asked.

"Oh, Leela, he was talking about going to see a lady doctor for marriage. I came back home and packed."

Raman arose from his meal and joined them. Leela had

181

told him about Julia and Selvam. "Why are you leaving so soon?" he asked. "Do not let Joseph frighten you away like this."

"I don't think I could bear to see him again," said Julia. "I must go now, tonight."

"It is understandable," said Leela, giving Julia a hug. "I hoped you could stay with us at least a few more days. Are you sure there is no hope?"

Julia exhaled. "Yes, it's better this way. Could you ask Arul to drive me to the train station?"

"We will drive you," said Raman. "We can get the jeep from Arul."

"At least have dinner with us first," said Leela.

Raman looked worried. "It is not good for you to take the night train. You will not be able to get a sleeper or a reserved seat at this time. I will have to find a place for you in the ladies' compartment."

Julia ate dinner with them as they discussed plans for her departure, and made sure they had her address in America. She promised to come and visit them when she had saved up enough money. Somehow she didn't feel as bad about leaving them as she had thought she would. They would always be a part of her life through letters and visits, as if she were simply their grown-up daughter who had moved away from home.

It was the thought of leaving Selvam that made it hard for her to eat or think. She couldn't imagine life without his continual overbearing presence, his fierce kisses, and his mischievously gleaming eyes. He had a way of being so impetuous at times, that she imagined him following her to Madras and laying all his mother's jewels at her feet to cajole her into staying with him . . . as his keep, of course. That image made Julia choke on her food.

Through her coughing she said, "You must not tell Selvam I've left."

"Certainly," said Leela. "But he will notice you are missing."

"Then tell him I've gone on a tour around India. Most of the Peace Corps workers are planning that. I think they've already gone. Yes, tell him I've gone with Harry. I'll get my ticket changed for the earliest possible date. Then even if he comes to the airport on Sunday, I'll be gone."

Leela and Raman agreed to her plan, and Julia felt a great wave of relief. She felt free of him, finally free.

But the feeling lasted only a short while. During the long eight-hour ride to Madras on the local train, which seemed to stop at every village and hamlet, she felt like a fugitive. She did feel guilty for not giving him a final farewell. And then she hadn't said good-bye to Dr. Arokiaswamy or anyone else. She had fled.

At Madras she checked into the Queen's Palace Hotel. In a way, by staying there, it was like being with Selvam for the last time, for that was where they had first met. She smiled sadly as she walked through the lobby. Who would have ever thought that the roguish sailor in the doorway, who had made her so upset that day, would have made her love him so completely?

Oh, Selvam, she sighed to herself, while in her imagination she raked her fingers through his thick hair, black as the blackest, moonless night. Then, looking at the door where he had stood, she remembered how later he had asked her to go to that room with him. The smile on her lips turned to angry firmness. From the beginning his intentions had been completely dishonorable.

Since it was only six thirty in the morning, she had to wait a few hours for the downtown airline office to open.

She went to a restaurant and had a breakfast of *puris* —delicious deep-fried unleavened bread—and a potato, pea, and onion dish. The cold humidity from the malfunctioning air conditioner felt worse than the heat outside. Nevertheless she savored every minute and every final experience of what would probably be her last day or so in India.

The exact time she had remaining was decided at the airline office after breakfast. They couldn't book her on that day's flight, but they did have openings for the following day. As the beautiful, olive-skinned secretary made the bookings for her, Julia admired her ornate gold button earrings with umbrella-shaped *jimikkis* dangling from them. Nirmala would have turned up her nose at such a traditional style, but the earrings did look quite chic on the secretary.

Julia wondered if Selvam's mother's collection contained earrings of a similar style—she hadn't seen any like them in the portion he had given Rita. She tried to dismiss the idea. How could she think of silly things like that when she was leaving the man she loved, the man she would always love. But she was obsessed with the earrings. They became an emblem of India to her, and of the life she might have had as Selvam's wife.

With her new airline ticket tucked safely in an inside compartment of her purse, she combed over several jewelry stores in the city until she found a gold earring-*jimikki* set similar to the one the airline secretary had worn. It took one hundred and ninety-six dollars out of her remaining three hundred dollars in traveler's checks to purchase it.

In her hotel room she put on the earrings. She felt it would be like taking a part of India home with her. But her satisfaction didn't last long. By six in the evening she decided she would have to phone Selvam and speak to him for the last time. She wouldn't tell him her whereabouts. She could keep up the pretense that she had gone on a tour. But she had to hear his voice one last time.

The hotel manager graciously left the office while she placed the call. Her heartbeat quickened as the phone at Dr. Arokiaswamy's house rang. She waited. It kept ringing and ringing. It seemed odd that no one answered it. At least Mrs. Arokiaswamy should be there. She rarely went out. And if she did go to visit with some women, at least the men would be at home.

Then suddenly it came to Julia, and she slowly replaced the receiver. They were out seeing girls, arranging marriage for Selvam with some lady doctor—Rani Rattanaswamy, Mrs. Arokiaswamy had said.

From then on Julia felt at a loss. She went to her room and bathed. Then she changed into a frilly sundress— yellow with pin-size polka dots. Aunt Frances used to say, "When you're down, dress up."

Although with the earrings and dress she looked ready for a poolside cocktail party, she didn't even feel like leaving the room. She had to force herself to go to the dining room and order dinner. Then she hardly touched it. She sat there for several hours ordering Limca and Fanta, drinking with a loose, bewildered expression on her face.

At ten o'clock a thin, barefooted servant came and informed her in his delicate voice that the dining room was about to close. Julia said she wanted to stay a little longer and would turn out the lights when she left. After the servant departed, she sat alone. The large room, which perhaps had been a ballroom very long ago, filled with a hollow quietness.

When she heard footsteps approaching her table a few

185

minutes later, she thought it might be the clerk to throw her out.

"Miss Julia, may I have this dance with you?" The voice was gentle with a deep resonance—and very familiar.

Julia looked up at Selvam's smiling face. He wore his navy blue suit, a gray silk shirt and pearl-white tie, pinned with a sparkling diamond. In a daze Julia stood up, protesting with a whimper, "But there's no music." She didn't know what else to say or do, so stunned she was by a flood of confused emotions.

"Then we'll imagine our own music," said Selvam. "What would the lady prefer?"

"A Strauss waltz," said Julia without deliberation. She slowly came to her senses and smiled back at Selvam.

"Would the Blue Danube do?" asked Selvam, as he took her out onto the dance floor and held her in waltz position. "It's the only one I can ever remember very well."

"It'll do quite well," said Julia, overwhelmed by his one hand firmly pressing on her back, and the other clasping her hand. She looked up at his sensual lips, black hair, and leaf-shaped dark eyes with their watery sparkle.

Selvam hummed the first few bars of the Blue Danube to establish the beat, then he pulled Julia into a fast, whirling waltz. She could hear the orchestra in her mind. The room spun around and around until she felt tingly with dizziness. It seemed she might fall, but she placed all her confidence in Selvam, in the strength of his arms and the solid weight of his body. He wouldn't let her fall. She knew that.

After a few minutes they stopped dancing. Selvam locked his hands loosely around her lower back and looked down at her with serious, brooding eyes. "Do you love me, Julia?"

Julia lowered her eyes. "Yes, I love you," she said meekly.

"My darling Julia." He kissed her on the forehead. "Leela told me everything—that you thought I wanted you for my keep, that you had run away to Madras. She also told me how much you love me, how you had confided that in her. But why didn't you tell me all this earlier?"

Julia looked back up at Selvam. She felt betrayed. "She promised not to tell you," she said weakly, ignoring his question. "Why did she? How could she?" Now that Selvam had come, Julia could not leave him again, and it was Leela's fault that he had found her.

Selvam's smile revealed his strong white teeth. "I think it was after I brought Dr. Rani Rattanaswamy to the clinic today." Selvam smiled at Julia while she tensed at hearing that name.

"Dr. Rattanaswamy," continued Selvam, "is a forty-one-year-old widow, quite plump, and with huge buck teeth. An excellent doctor, highly recommended."

With great difficulty Julia asked, "But aren't you planning to marry her?"

"No, my dearest. How could I think of marrying anyone else but you? I love you so much, there could never be another woman for me. But I didn't know until today that you truly love me too. Oh, I knew there was physical attraction, but I needed to know that you love me."

"I do love you. I love you so much, it tore me apart."

His voice filled with anguish. "My Julia, if I'd only known that you misunderstood. I should have thought something was wrong, but I was so preoccupied with Rita's marriage."

He paused. His gaze held hers. "Believe me, I never intended to make you my keep."

187

"Then why did you want me to read *Shilappadikaram*, about a courtesan dancing girl."

"No, Julia. I think you didn't read the whole book."

"I was so upset by what I thought was your intention."

"I wanted you to read it because it's one of the greatest works of Tamil literature. I wanted to share it with you. And it's not about Madhavi, the courtesan, but about Kannaki, the faithful Tamil wife and daughter-in-law, who remains loyal through all problems. I also thought it would please *cinnamma* if you read it."

He looked away for a moment, then looked back at her with painful intensity. "Can't you see how much I hate the very idea of having a mistress after what my father and mother went through? And I never wanted an arranged marriage. I always knew that I'd have to have a love marriage. Perhaps Leela guessed it, and that's why she worked so hard to bring us together."

He brought his hands to her face, cupping it and stroking it with his thumbs, while he examined her closely. "I need to be very sure of the love on both sides, because there will be only one woman for me for the rest of my life—the woman I love and marry. But I couldn't speak of marriage to you until I was certain you loved me. And I couldn't bring it up to my parents, not until it was certain between us. I just wanted to give you as much time as possible, so you'd know for sure." He bent down and kissed her firmly.

A current of desire flowed through Julia as his lips demanded her response. When at last the kiss ended, she said, "I think I started falling in love with you right here, when we first met. I didn't know it then. I thought I hated you because you disturbed me so much. And then after we had worked together I knew I loved you. But I thought

188

your motives were . . . When you asked me to come to your hotel room that day we first met . . ."

"Oh, that." Selvam laughed. He again held her loosely around the waist. "Leela had written so much about you, but I had to find out for myself. I think if you had come with me I would have dropped all intentions of marriage. As it was, you beguiled me by your aloofness." A mischievous look spread over his face. "And now, my Julia, I'm asking you once more to come to my room."

Julia's body stiffened instinctively and Selvam sensed it. With his eyes twinkling he asked, "Don't you trust me now?"

Julia quivered, but she said with confidence, "Yes, Selvam, I trust you now."

"Good! Everyone's there—*cinnamma, appa,* Leela, Ramanathan, Nirmala and Rita and their husbands. But we have to wait here a few more minutes while they prepare for the engagement ceremony. I insisted that we be engaged immediately."

He looked at her with longing, then added with a prayerlike softness, "My family was very pleased I chose to marry you. *Appa* was also pleased when I told him I planned to take over his practice at the clinic."

"And your father—you're not angry with him?"

"No, of course not. I was hurt as a child, but long ago I forgave him. Before coming here Leela explained about my father and mother. I was glad to have a better understanding, but somehow she'd mistakenly thought I was bitter."

"Then you planned all along to stay at the clinic?" Julia looked at him with surprise.

Selvam's voice increased to a confident tone. "Of course. I closed my practice and sent all my belongings by sea mail. They should be arriving in a few weeks. But after

I met you in Madras and decided you were the girl I wanted to marry, I thought it best to let *appa* think I was planning to go back to America. I knew how much he wanted me to stay. Then when I was going to tell him I wanted to marry you, I was going to throw in my plan to stay here—as part of the bargain, so to speak. But in the end he didn't need any such convincing. My parents both are very fond of you."

Julia smiled. Not only would she marry the man she loved, but his family had accepted her. It seemed a miracle all this was happening after suffering so much under false impressions. "Selvam, I'm so glad you came. I'm so glad your family . . ." She started to cry, then with a quavering voice she changed the topic to the practical matters at hand. "Now, what about the engagement ceremony? I never attended one. Is there anything I have to know?"

"The two mothers have the largest parts." He smiled down at her and jostled her slightly in his arms. "You'll be the centerpiece, all decorated with flowers and jewelry. *Cinnamma* and Leela will coach you along. My presence isn't even required. The groom doesn't have any part in this ceremony, but I wouldn't miss it for the world. I'll sneak in and watch my beloved Julia becoming engaged to me."

"And Leela will take the part of my mother?"

"Yes. She already has tears in her eyes about marrying you off."

Selvam kissed her again on the forehead. "Would it be all right, Julia, to have our wedding during this marriage season? There are still a few more weeks before *adi masam*. Otherwise we'd have to wait until after *adi* and I don't want to wait any longer than necessary."

"Yes." Julia's eyes gleamed brightly. Now that her

misunderstanding was cleared, she, too, felt impatient to be his, completely his.

"Good, then later on you, Nirmala, and Rita can all have a joint ceremony to change the *tali* from the cotton string to the gold chain."

Julia listened, enraptured with visions of their happiness together. Selvam continued, "Of course, I'll also give you a wedding ring for our trips to America. I want to take you there for our honeymoon. I want you to meet my host family."

"Your host family?"

"The Reynoldses, in Los Angeles. I lived with them the first year I was in America. Dr. Reynolds is an English professor."

"Who specializes in poetry, no doubt." Julia smiled broadly.

"Yes, that's right." Selvam also smiled. "And we'll want to visit your aunt and uncle."

"Yes, I want to see them very much now." Julia's voice again trembled. "I know they were never like parents to me, but then I suppose I was never like a daughter to them."

"Julia," asked Selvam, becoming serious, "do you mind wearing a *tali* and having a *tali*-tying ceremony during the wedding? Not for me, but my family would be pleased."

"Oh, Selvam, you don't know how much I'd like to wear your *tali*." She closed her eyes, holding back her tears of happiness.

"Then you must wear it always. It's the symbol of your husband." His eyes twinkled with merriment.

Julia smiled, then reached up and kissed him lightly on the cheek. "It'll be very precious to me."

He pulled her into his arms and held her head against his shoulder. His voice became a whisper. "All the women will be fluttering around us with their ceremonies and fuss. We won't get much chance to be alone again until we're married. . . ."

There's always the beach, she thought with her own mischievous smile, as Selvam tilted her head back with his large, strong hands. Then his lips descended forcefully to hers. She closed her eyes and yielded completely to the sweetness and passion of the moment.